Holly's First Love

Other books by Beverly Lewis:

Secret Summer Dreams
Sealed with a Kiss
The Trouble with Weddings

Holly's First Love

BEVERLY ♥ LEWIS

ZondervanPublishingHouse
Grand Rapids, Michigan

A Division of HarperCollins*Publishers*

Y
F
Lew

To Dave Lewis,
My Heart-Mate

♥ Author's Note ♥

Hugs go to my terrific teen consultants—Niki, Julie, Janie, Amy, Allison, and Becky.

My Monday night SCBWI group—including Mary Erickson, Vicki Fox, Peggy Marshall, and Carol Reinsma—offered valuable assistance on the manuscript. So did Barbara Birch, Barbara Reinhard, and my husband, Dave.

I'm grateful to Dave Lambert, who believed in Holly Heart from the start, and to my editor Lori Walburg for her encouragement, hard work, and yes . . . giggles!

Thanks to Del Gariepy, who shared his medical expertise.

ONE

"Is it hot in here?" I whispered to the boy sharing my music folder.

Tom Sly's eyes bulged. "Holly Meredith, you're green!"

Halfway through our seventh grade musical, on the second riser, in front of half the population of Dressel Hills, Colorado—it happened. Faces in the audience began to blur. Heat rushed to my throbbing head. With a mouth drier than Arizona, I gasped for breath. Then my knees buckled and . . . I blacked out!

My best friend, Andrea (Andie) Martinez, witnessed this embarrassing scene and filled me in on the details later. She jumped off the risers, hightailing it over to help me. Tom Sly dragged me behind the risers and across the newly-waxed gym floor to the janitor's room. Jared Wilkins followed.

When I came to, I was lying on the floor in the musty janitor's room. The first thing I saw was the adorable face of Jared Wilkins, the new boy. He smiled down at me, fanning me back to life with his music folder. In my half-dazed state, his blue eyes seemed to dance dreamily. *Maybe this fainting stuff isn't so bad after all*, I thought, squinting through the blurry haze.

"Holly," Jared said. "Can you hear me?"

"Uh-huh," I whispered.

"Hang in there. Andrea went to get your mom." He glanced at Tom Sly, who leaned against the doorway, fidgeting.

Jared helped me sit up next to some mops and a bucket. I still felt a little dizzy, but not so bad that I couldn't enjoy being the focus of his attention.

"Are you feeling okay?" he asked.

"I think so," I said weakly.

"That's good. You just take it easy till your mom gets here, all right?" Smiling, he sat beside me, leaning against the wall. "What a smooth way to get out of a boring musical!"

"Speak for yourself," I said, feeling a bit stronger. "You didn't just faint in front of thousands of people."

"But it's very romantic, being rescued by two men, don't you think?"

I was about to tell him that two seventh-grade boys didn't exactly qualify as men, but just then Mom and my little sister Carrie burst into the room, followed by Andie.

"Holly, honey, are you all right?" Mom touched

my forehead while Carrie hugged me around the waist.

"I think she's okay," Jared said, smiling at me. "It just got a little too *hot* up on stage."

"Well, let's get you out of this musty mess and into some fresh air," Mom said. "Thank you for your help, boys."

"No problem," Jared said. Tom gave me a weird grin.

Mom led me down the hallway and settled me into a chair in an empty classroom. Then she and Carrie went to search for a glass of water. As soon as they were out of earshot, Andie sat next to me. She twisted one of her short curls around her finger. When she does that I know something's up!

"Holly," she whispered, "you'll never guess what happened when you were knocked out."

"What?" I asked, still feeling a bit woozy.

"One of the boys tried to give you mouth-to-mouth resuscitation."

"What?" Suddenly wide awake, I grabbed Andie's arm. *"Who* did?"

Andie shook her head and looked away. "I, uh, shouldn't tell you."

"What do you mean *shouldn't?*"

"Oh, Holly," she whined. "I shouldn't have said anything."

I grabbed her other arm. "I *have* to know!"

She pulled away from me. "Don't do this, Holly."

"Do what? We're best friends, remember?"

She folded her arms. "I can't tell you."

"Why not?" I was desperate. "Did his lips actually touch mine?"

Andie nodded solemnly.

"Ewww!" I groaned.

"Your first kiss, and you weren't even awake for it," Andie said.

"Andie!" I howled. "Who was it?"

I was about ready to shake the answer out of her when Andie's parents poked their heads in the door. "Ready to go, Andie?" Mrs. Martinez asked. "We told the baby-sitter we'd be back by nine."

"Okay, Mom," Andie called. Then she whispered to me, "Call me the second you get home."

"You can count on it," I said.

Mom returned with a glass of water and made me drink it. Then she held my arm while we walked to the car. Carrie opened the door for me. During the drive home, Mom kept pampering me.

"Are you feeling better, Holly-Heart?" she asked. Flicking on the inside light, she stroked the top of my head. "The color's returned to your cheeks. That's good."

Carrie giggled from the back seat. "You looked like a ghost up there."

"Did I? Did everybody see me faint?" I was mortified. Not only had I been kissed by a boy while unconscious, but a whole auditorium full of parents and kids had watched me keel over!

"Now, Holly, things like this can happen to anyone," Mom said. "There's nothing to be embarrassed about."

"But Mom, that's not *all* that happened," I said. Then I told her about the near-resuscitation.

I could tell she was trying to hide a smile. But all she said was, "A little kiss won't hurt you, Holly." Carrie just stared at me with bug eyes.

"But Andie won't tell me who it was! I'd love it if it was Jared, but if it was Tom Sly—"

Mom couldn't hide her smile any longer. "Does Jared happen to be the cute new boy you've been raving about? The one who spoke to me?"

I nodded. Carrie caught on and chanted, "Holly and Jared, sit-tin' in a tree, K-I-S-S-I-N-G—"

"Mom!" I protested, staring at Carrie. I didn't need trouble from my eight-year-old sister, too.

"Carrie, be still," Mom said. Carrie giggled, then covered her mouth when Mom glared at her in the rearview mirror.

We pulled into the driveway, and Mom pressed the garage door opener. I could hear the phone ringing as we got out of the car.

"It's Andie!" I said. "Hurry and open the door!"

I made a mad dash for the phone. "Hello?" I said.

It *was* Andie. "What took so long?"

"Nothing," I said. "We came right home." Good thing we had a cordless phone. I retreated to my favorite telephone stall—the downstairs bathroom. No one could hear me there. I lowered the toilet lid and settled down.

"Okay, now tell me," I said.

She told me what happened when I blacked

11

out—everything except the kiss. Then she said, "What do *you* remember about tonight?"

I told her everything except the most private moments with Jared.

"That's it?" she asked.

"Yes!" I said impatiently. "Now when are you going to tell me who kissed me?"

She sighed. "Like I said, I can't tell you, Holly."

"Why not?" I demanded.

"Honestly," she said, "I wouldn't keep my best friend in the dark unless—"

"Unless what?"

"Unless it's for her own good."

"Don't make me crazy, Andie. What good is not knowing?"

"My lips are sealed. True friends must shield one another sometimes."

"C'mon, don't get weird, Andie. Tell me!"

"I can't, I really can't."

"Okay, I'll ask Jared. He'll tell me the truth."

"That's not a good idea," she said.

"Why not? He was there, he should know."

"You're getting hyper, Holly."

"Of course I am!" I was ready to pull my hair out. "Look, Andie, I'm not going to talk to you till you tell me who kissed me."

"But—"

"Good-bye, Andie." What a nightmare. The most important thing that had ever happened to me, and my own best friend wouldn't talk about it!

TWO

Luckily I had two whole days to get over my fainting episode. I would have died of embarrassment if I had to go to school the very next day!

I spent Saturday morning writing in my diary. Ever since third grade, I'd kept a journal. My secret wish was to be a writer when I grew up. If I ever made it through seventh grade.

My hand shook as I wrote the date: Saturday, January 16. Then I described the whole humiliating evening. Right down to Andie's awful secret. What had happened while I lay there, dead to the world? I imagined several scenarios and wrote them down. In one scene, Jared pressed his lips to mine and I woke up at his touch. In another, Tom tried to kiss me and Jared bravely pushed him away, protecting my innocent lips.

Carrie called up the stairs, interrupting my thoughts. "Holly! Andie's on the phone for you."

"Tell her I'm busy," I yelled back.

"She won't believe it!" she said.

I went to the head of the stairs. "Tell her I'm out."

"No, you're not."

"Okay!" I said, exasperated. "This is the truth: Tell her I won't talk to her until she tells me in person what happened last night."

"All right!" Carrie said.

I went downstairs and watched her tell Andie what I'd said. After she hung up I asked, "What'd she say?"

" 'Over my dead body,' " Carrie repeated, snickering.

I tromped back to my room. Enough of Andie's nonsense! "This means war," I muttered.

I made a point of snubbing Andie at church the next day. My conscience hurt a little when the minister talked about forgiveness, but I tried to forget about it. I was still too upset.

At school on Monday, hoping to talk to Jared or Tom, I arrived early to Miss Wannamaker's gloomy English classroom. The walls were a sick grey, a sorry color for a room where some of my best creative writing happened—assigned by one of my favorite teachers. Miss W was one of the fattest people I'd ever seen. But she had the face of an angel and the heart of a saint.

The classroom slowly filled, but before I could catch either Jared or Tom, Miss W herself came in.

"Dear class," she began, like a letter. That was her way. Every day. "Let's turn to page 249 in your literature books." She faced the chalkboard and wrote a "pithy" quotation, as she called it. The flap of skin under her arm jiggled as she wrote.

"Hey, Jared. How much to call Miss W the 'B' word?" Tom Sly whispered behind me. I glanced at Jared, who sat across the aisle.

"What do you mean? *Blob*?" Jared blurted out.

Miss W whirled around. "Jared. Tom." They looked up, shocked. "You will see me after class."

Her tone meant trouble—*big* trouble. I didn't feel sorry for Tom. His show-off routine had finally caught up with him. But Jared? That was another story . . .

Two months ago, right before Thanksgiving, Jared Wilkins had moved to Dressel Hills, our ski village nestled in the Colorado Rockies. I often caught him watching me. Of course, I sent zillions of encouraging glances right back. I secretly hoped *he* was the one who had come to my rescue last night . . . kissing me back to life like some fairy tale prince.

"Dear class," Miss W said again. "I'm returning the quizzes from last week."

The papers came around. I got a ninety percent—not bad for last-minute cramming.

"Now for Thursday's assignment," she said. We all groaned, but she ignored us. "I would like you to write a short story, with a two-page minimum." More groans. "The main character must have something in common with yourself. Either your

15

personality, hobby, or a special interest. Other-wise, the sky's the limit."

I jotted notes in my red spiral and sneaked a look at Jared. He gestured that we should talk after class. I smiled yes.

Out of the corner of my eye, I saw Andie scrunch her eyes at me like a snapping turtle ready to attack. I turned my back and ignored her. True to my word, I hadn't spoken to her all day—even though her locker was right next to mine.

After English, Miss W scolded Jared and Tom. I waited in the hallway, nervously twisting my hair. Who should I ask about Friday night? Jared or Tom? Tom was a tease and a real pain, but at least I'd known him since first grade. I hardly knew Jared at all. Finally, I decided to play it by ear.

Before long, Jared came out. "Hope you aren't in trouble," I said.

"Not really, but Tom's still in there," he said. We started down the hall towards our lockers. "Are you going to the youth meeting tomorrow night?" he asked.

"Pastor Rob wants us to wait till we're thirteen to join," I said, my heart thump-thumping.

"Really? When will that be?" He reached for my books.

"You won't believe it if I tell you." I was actually walking down the corridors of Dressel Hills Junior High with the best-looking guy in school balancing my books on his hip!

"Try me."

"February 14."

He looked surprised. "Valentine's Day?"

"That's right." My face felt like a bad sunburn. Jared must've noticed. He winked, which made it worse.

"How'd you get a Christmasy name like Holly?" Not waiting for the answer, he added, "Sweetheart fits much better."

What was wrong with my knees? They shook like I was up on the second riser again . . .

"My mom named me after her great aunt," I said. "We share the same name, but that's where the similarity ends."

"What do you mean?"

"She became a missionary to Africa."

"Really?"

"Her life was filled with fabulous excitement— dangerous adventure that would build your faith instantly. *I'm* lucky if I remember to read my devotions every day."

Jared grinned.

"Mom calls me Holly-Heart," I volunteered without thinking. "It's her special nickname for me, because of my Valentine birthday."

"It's perfect for you. You *are* all heart, aren't you?" His eyes softened.

I didn't dare tell him the nickname my gym teacher had chosen for me. Holly-bones was verbal abuse at its worst, I thought, tucking my shirt into the tiny waist of my light blue jeans.

Arriving at my locker, we found Andie rummaging in hers.

"See you tomorrow," Jared said, handing back my books.

"Okay." My heart pounded as he headed down the hall.

"Sounds promising," Andie muttered inside her messy locker.

Refusing to say anything, I spun my combination lock and opened the door—right into Andie's.

"Ex-cuse me!" Andie said, pushing my door aside. Then she slammed her locker shut and stomped off.

I shrugged. I was going to show Andie I meant business. No way would I let her withhold valuable information from me—her best friend.

Suddenly, Tom was beside me, hanging on my locker door. "That was some act you pulled off last Friday night," he teased. "One way to upstage the entire seventh grade."

"I suppose," I said, rummaging around my locker as if I were trying to find something. Now was my chance to ask, but did I dare?

"You were so wiped out," he said, like he was dying to talk about it.

I summoned up my courage. "What happened after I fainted?" I asked. I kept my head in my locker so he couldn't see my flaming face.

"You mean Andie didn't tell you?" he said.

"No."

"*Ve-ry* interesting," he said, putting his hand to his chin and stroking an imaginary beard. "Well, I guess you'll never know then, huh? See you, Holly." He waved and took off down the hall.

Weird, I thought. Why wouldn't he tell me? Well, that left Jared. Now I'd *have* to ask him.

I walked home, watching my breath float ahead of me. As usual, Dressel Hills was swarming with winter tourists. Skiers roamed the streets and crowded into the shops and coffee houses. I turned the corner away from the bustling village, towards Downhill Court. The trees, bare as skeletons, shivered in the cold mountain air.

Picking my way along the slippery street, I thought of Jared. Could someone so good-looking really like me? Could he overlook my "no-shape" and see my heart instead? Daddy had with Mom. She was so thin when they met, he said she looked like a pipe cleaner in her furry coat. As for me, I ate like a hippo, but nothing changed. Something about my metabolism made me burn up the fat. Meanwhile, all the other girls were changing . . . developing. Maybe something would happen in time for my thirteenth birthday—twenty-seven eternal days from now.

I waved to a neighbor and plodded ahead to the tri-level three houses away. Flecks of powdery snow dusted the bricked icy walkway. I hoped we'd have another snow day soon. Andie and I always managed to get together, no matter how bad the streets were.

Then I remembered—she and I weren't talking. I kicked at the hardened grey clump of ice clinging to the gutter in front of our house. This secrecy stuff made me mad. I *had* to get Andie to talk.

When I walked in the front door, Mom was

19

relaxing with her usual after-work cup of pepper-mint tea. I pulled off my shoes.

"Love you, Mom," I said, tossing my scarf aside.

"Everything okay at school?" She sipped her tea.

I dumped my books on the sofa, scaring Goofey, our cat, away. "Andie's a total nightmare."

"What do you mean, Holly-Heart?"

"She *still* won't tell me who kissed me Friday night." I pressed my hands against my cold face. "Mom, I've *got* to know who it was."

She nodded.

"I tried to ask Tom, but he wouldn't tell either."

"What are you going to do now?" Mom asked.

"I don't know," I said glumly.

Three whole days had passed since I back-flipped off the risers, and Andie still guarded her secret. I wondered if she'd paid the boys to keep their mouths shut. Sooner or later the truth had to pop out. Whatever it was.

THREE

After school the next day I studied at the library while I waited for Jared to get out of basketball practice. For once I didn't have to go home to be with Carrie, because she was going to a friend's house after school.

I couldn't exactly study, though. I kept looking out the window, across to the gym. I pictured Jared shooting baskets and dribbling up and down the court. I hoped I could muster up the nerve to ask him who kissed me!

Just then I spied Jared leaving the gym, wearing gray sweats, his navy blue gym bag slung over his shoulder. Even with his hair wet from the shower, he looked fine. I jumped up and was out the front doors of the school in a shot.

Jared waved, coming across the freshly-plowed walkway towards me.

"Hi, Holly. Glad you waited." He grinned, like he was *really* glad. He held the door for me as we went back into the building. "Time for a coke?"

"Sure." *Thump-thumpity* went my heart.

"Wish you didn't have to wait another month to come to the youth meetings. I'll miss seeing you there tonight."

I breathed slower, deeper. *Should I ask him about Andie's secret now?*

We stopped at his locker. I waited while he grabbed his jacket and books. It was now or never.

I took a deep breath. "Jared, uh, can I ask you something personal?"

"Sure, anything."

"I'm having a little trouble getting things straight."

He closed his locker and leaned against it. Close to me. "What things?"

"Like what happened, you know, Friday night when I fainted?"

Right then Andie appeared.

She marched straight towards us like a soldier ready for war. Her dark eyes flashed. I tried to ignore her, but she came right up to me.

"Holly, can I talk to you a minute?" she asked, oh-so-sweetly. She flashed a smile at Jared.

I was trapped. I couldn't be rude to her in front of Jared. What would he think?

"Excuse me, Jared," I said. "Can you wait here?"

"No problem. Take your time."

I pulled her over to our lockers. I had vowed not

22

to speak to her, and I wasn't about to now. She'd just have to read my looks.

"Are you crazy?" she asked.

I shrugged and reached into my locker for my coat.

"Cut the jokes. Don't talk to Jared," she said.

I scowled at her as I pulled my hair out of my coat collar and flung it over my shoulder.

"Talk to *me*," her voice softened. "We're best friends."

My patience with her was almost gone. I glanced down the hall at Jared, who was still waiting. It was useless. I had to talk.

"Look, Andie," I hissed, "you've played your secretive game too long."

"Have you forgotten our Loyalty Papers?" she demanded.

"'Course not," I said. "After all, *I* wrote most of them." In third grade Andie and I had drawn up our first Loyalty Papers. Every possible problem in our friendship had been thought out carefully and written down, legal-like. "Devoted, caring best friends, until the final end of us," were some of its dramatic words. We revised the Loyalty Papers every year. But the message always remained the same—pals to the very end.

"Well, you're not following them, are you?" she said, looking up at me. The top of her dark head barely reached my shoulders.

"Hey, Holly!" Jared waved from down the hall. "I can just meet you at the Soda Straw later, okay?"

23

"Okav!" I waved back. "I'll be there in a minute As soon as I knew he was out of earshot, I turned on Andie. "You're spoiling everything," I said. "Listen here, Andie, if you hadn't shown up just now, I'd know who kissed me the other night."

"Not kissed," she said, "artificially resuscitated."

"Whatever."

She yanked all the junk out of her locker and began hurling books to the floor. It looked like the beginning of one of her fits. "I can't believe you asked him," she said over her shoulder. "You should reread our Loyalty Papers."

"I don't see what our Loyalty Papers have to do with this," I said. "If you'd stop being so stubborn and just tell me—"

"Look who's being stubborn!" Andie interrupted.

"I should have known better than to talk to you." I slammed my locker extra hard and stomped off. Andie was being totally unreasonable, and I wasn't going to put up with it anymore.

Outside, the mountain air cooled me down some, but I was still steaming inside. Andie had never been so rude before, and we'd been friends for ten years—ever since preschool, where we became instant playmates. By first grade we were true-blue, best friends, and that's how it had been ever since. We even traded favorite teddy bears! Her droopy-eyed Bearie-O had been sitting on *my* bed for six years. My hugging had worn the tan fur

24

off his teddy head. And my beloved Corky sat with a collection of stuffed animals in *her* room.

Maybe it's time to send Bearie-O back, I thought as I opened the jingling door to the Soda Straw. It was a fifties-style diner, with red vinyl booths, stools lined up at the aluminum counter, and a jukebox in the corner.

Jared sat in a booth towards the back of the restaurant, his notebook spread out in front of him. My heart did its skippy thing.

He looked up as I slid into the seat opposite him. "Still thirsty?" he asked, his eyes twinkling.

"Sure," I said. When the waitress came around, I ordered a coke.

Jared leaned forward, tapping his pen on the table. "Where were we, before, uh—"

"Oh, sorry about that," I interrupted. "Thanks for waiting for me."

"Wouldn't have missed *this* for anything."

I felt my face grow hot. "Doing homework?"

"Just plotting my short story for English. Have you written yours?"

"Not yet." I couldn't tell him my mind had been focused on more important things . . . like him.

"I was worried about you the other night. Hope you didn't hurt yourself when you fell," he said softly.

"There aren't any bruises." The waitress brought my coke in a tall soda glass.

"Glad I could help." Jared closed his notebook.

I sipped some pop. "Was I breathing?"

"You were breathing okay."

"Then why did I need mouth-to-mouth resuscitation?"

"Oh, you heard about that?"

Br-ring! The bell on the door jingled as Andie appeared, popping my magical moment. Again!

"Hi, guys!" she called, bouncing over to our table.

Couldn't she read the secret message in my eyes? *Get lost. Get lost.*

Jared looked surprised. Her timing was unbelievable.

"Hi, I'm Andie Martinez," she said to Jared. "We met when Holly, uh, fainted the other night." She tipped an invisible hat.

"You two must be friends," Jared said, looking at me.

I wanted to say no, but told the truth. "We're best friends."

"Can I borrow her again?" Andie asked.

"We were just leaving," he said.

"Oh, were you headed somewhere?" she asked, her voice honey-sweet. Sickeningly sweet.

"Nowhere," I said. *Thanks to you.*

Awkwardly, Jared and I stood up. Looking into his face, I realized we were almost the same height.

Andie grabbed my arm. "I need to see you, Holly. Alone." She mumbled something to Jared about being sorry and escorted me out the door and over to a clump of aspen trees. I was ready for a face-off like in ice hockey, only this was a game I wanted to end.

"What are you doing?" I demanded.

"What's it look like? I'm ready to talk. To fill you in on what happened Friday night."

"I don't believe it! You've finally come to your senses." I glanced back at the Soda Straw. "So, talk."

"This is it—the truth. Jared didn't try to revive you. *Tom* did."

I heard her words, but they didn't make sense. I wanted to turn her upside-down like a salt shaker to get all the answers out.

"Why didn't you tell me this in the first place?" I tried to erase the mental picture of Tom leaning over me, his breath on mine.

"You really shouldn't be so curious, Holly."

"Andie, give me a break."

"Figure it out," she said, her nose red from the cold. "We're in love with the same guy."

"What?" I exclaimed. "Jared?"

She nodded.

"No wonder you're following us around everywhere," I said. "It's disgusting."

"Don't change the subject. There's more," she said, surprisingly eager to tell me everything. "Jared grabbed Tom off the floor—away from you."

Just as I had imagined it in my diary! "Really? What did he say?"

"His exact words: 'Get up, you total jerk!'"

"He said *that*?"

"Jared knew you didn't need artificial resuscitation. You were *breathing*. Tom jumped at the chance to get next to your lips," she said, studying me.

I wiped my lips on my coat sleeve, groaning. "I was probably his first kiss."

"Maybe, maybe not."

"So, you kept that part a big secret—about Jared pulling Tom away. Because you didn't want me to know how Jared feels about me. Right?"

"That's it," she said. "It's just that I wanted Jared to like *me*. Am I forgiven?"

"If you promise me one thing," I said.

"What?"

"Ban the secrets, okay?"

"I promise. No secrets. But I can't promise much else." I knew what *that* meant. The battle lines had been drawn. Jared was fair game. Not surprisingly, Andie and I had more in common than ever before. Only now instead of trading teddy bears, we were playing tug-of-war with a boy.

Jared burst out of the diner and waved to us. He crossed the snow-packed street to catch the city bus. We watched as the doors closed, sighing identical sighs. This was too much!

"I wonder if he needs a typist for his English assignment," Andie said, breaking the spell.

"You wouldn't dare!"

Our eyes locked. Better than anyone else, I knew Andie would do what she wanted. No one could talk her out of it. Not even her best friend.

"Well, I gotta go," Andie said. "Might need some typing paper. And then I have youth group tonight—with Jared. See you later, Holly." She walked off, her curls bouncing.

I watched her cross the street and go into a drugstore. Then, more angry and confused than ever, I headed for home. I wasn't quite sure what had just happened, but it seemed that I had traded the mini-problem of Andie's secret for a worse problem—the green-eyed monster. No way would I let Andie get Jared. No way!

FOUR

When I arrived home, Carrie met me at the door. "Hi, Holly," she said, looking up at me with pleading eyes. "Will you french braid my hair?"

I sighed. "Okay, but let me grab a snack first. Where's Mom?" I poured some pop and threw together a peanut butter sandwich.

Carrie sat at the kitchen counter and banged her legs impatiently against the stool. "She'll be down. She already drank her tea. Guess you missed it."

It meant the first half hour of Mom's arrival. She was usually cheerful even after a long day at work. But the peppermint tea was her thing. A way to unwind.

"How are my angels?" Mom said, coming downstairs. She was wearing the giant elephant slippers I had given her for Christmas.

"Hi, Mom." I hugged her. "You look tired."

"I guess I am a little." She sat on the sofa, handing a yellow flyer to me. "This came in the mail today from church. It's information about a teen choir audition. And they'll be traveling."

I clutched my throat—one of my dreams! "Do you think I could audition for it?"

"There's a good chance, honey. I'm sure the director will realize you're *almost* thirteen. Your birthday is so close." She flipped a page of the Psalms calendar on the lamp table. My birthday was marked with a red heart. It was going to be the best day of my life, if it ever arrived.

"When are the auditions?" I asked.

Carrie pulled me out of the living room, her pink brush and comb in her other hand.

"Next week Tuesday," Mom said.

"I'm definitely going to try out," I said.

"C'mon, Holly, braid my hair *now*," Carrie said.

I reached for her brush. "Okay, let's do it."

Andie and I had learned how to french braid in third grade. We'd visited her aunt's beauty salon one rainy day and had come home informed fashion critics.

Peering down at Carrie's thick golden locks, I remembered the first time I'd tried to braid her hair like this. It was four years ago, on the day Daddy moved out. Carrie was four, and I was eight.

I had helped carry Daddy's shoeboxes out to the car. I knew I shouldn't have tossed them in any-old-way. Lids and shoes scattered all over the back

31

seat. Some helper I was. Daddy frowned at me for throwing them in. I didn't care. That's how my insides felt . . . all scrambled up.

Inside the house, he put his arm around my shoulder. "Holly-Heart, you and Carrie can come visit me at my new place any time." With that, he kissed little Carrie and me.

"*This* is your place," I said. "And Mom's and mine and Carrie's!" It was weird—no one scolded me for yelling at him.

After Daddy closed the door behind him, I went over to Carrie, who sat huddled beside Mom on the couch. I took her hand. She followed me upstairs to the bathroom sink where I wet her hair and tried the first french braid. We could hear Mom's soft sobbing downstairs. *Things will never be the same*, I had thought. It was the worst day of my life.

"Make it tighter, so it won't come out." Carrie's voice pierced my thoughts. I pulled the strands carefully, making a perfect braid.

We didn't see Daddy after that. It frightened me. Things *weren't* the same. Eventually, though, things got better. Mom didn't cry so much anymore, and Carrie and I managed to survive without Daddy around.

"There you go." I finished off the braid with an elastic tie and a tiny ribbon. "You look fabulous."

Carrie ran downstairs to show Mom. I headed to my room to write the latest developments in my diary. Andie and I both after the same boy . . . that meant trouble ahead.

♥ ♥ ♥

During warm-ups in gym on Wednesday, Andie asked if I'd heard about the teen choir tryouts.

"Sounds exciting," I said.

"Pastor Rob told us about it after youth service last night." She fluffed her hair, then twisted a strand of it around her finger. A bad sign.

"Jared and I signed up to try out," she said. "Too bad you're too young."

She acted like they were going out already—just because they were both auditioning! "I'll be thirteen before the tour," I said. But I felt left out. What if I weren't allowed to audition—and Andie and Jared *did* go on the choir tour together? Andie would get Jared for sure.

We practiced lay-ups and Andie missed every time! When my turn came, I dribbled up and banked it in. There were a few advantages to being tall.

"Nice shot, Holly-bones!" Miss Neff shouted across the court.

There it was—the dreaded nickname. Half the class snickered. It was true. I was bony all right, and there was no hiding it. I tugged on the back of my green gym suit. My stork legs barely filled out the giant shorts. Mom had darted the suit to fit my waist, but she couldn't do anything about the hideous-looking wide-legged hems.

"Have you had your bacon and eggs today?" a curvaceous classmate joked as she dribbled past me down the court. I watched her move away

33

gracefully. *Someday*, I thought. *Someday I'll look like that*.

"Each of us has a body clock," Mom had explained last year when we had our first heart-to-heart talk about womanly things. Trouble was, *my* body clock seemed to be losing time.

"By the way," Andie mentioned after showers, "Jared doesn't need a typist. But he *does* need an accompanist for his choir audition."

I whirled around, towel and all. "You talked to him?" She was keeping her promise all right—no secrets. So how come it hurt when she told me everything?

"After the youth meeting last night. He wants me to play the piano for him." Andie swaggered around, emphasizing her excitement. And her shape.

I couldn't compete with a fabulous pianist. Andie was moving in . . . fast!

After school I raced to my room to start the creative writing assignment for English. I titled it, "Love Times Two." It was about fraternal twin sisters who had nothing in common except the love of their lives. I wasn't foolish enough to give them names like Holly and Andie, but *I* knew what the story was about, and so would Andie and Jared. But the story was safe, for Miss W's eyes only.

"Hi ya, Bearie-O," I said, picking up Andie's old teddy bear. "Depending on how things go with your owner, you might not be here much longer. But before you go, you have to hear my side of the story." I began reading my first draft out loud. Halfway through the second page, Mom called from downstairs.

"Holly-Heart, Andie is here."

"Send her up," I called.

Andie dashed up the steps and plopped down on my canopy bed, snuggling with Bearie-O. "Ready to launch a writing career?"

"A what?"

She slid a twenty-dollar bill out of her jeans. "You heard me."

I stared at the money. "What's that for?"

"For you, if you do a good job on my short story."

"You're joking, right?"

"Nope. I have to baby-sit my little brothers tonight. I don't have time to write it."

"I can't do that. It's dishonest."

"What'll I do? Miss W will hang me from the ceiling if I don't turn it in."

"Maybe, but it still beats lying," I said.

Peeking over my shoulder, she asked, "What's *your* masterpiece about?"

I shoved it safely into a folder. "You'll never know."

"You were reading it to Bearie-O, weren't you?"

"Sure, I tell him everything. Same as you—just not this."

"You're hopeless," she said pushing the twenty back inside her faded jeans.

"Pals forever?" I said with a shy grin.

"Some pal you are." She stood up to leave.

"At least I help keep you honest."

She scrunched up her face and said, "You really are Holly-Heartless." She closed my door with a thud.

Bearie-O took it all in. So did I. After all, I wasn't interfering with *her* first love. Just refusing to do her homework.

The next morning I hugged Mom before heading off for school. My clean hair smelled like roses under my knit hat. I couldn't wait to see Jared again. And to turn in my fabulous short story.

Finally, English class! I slid into my seat and pulled my fiction assignment out of its shiny red cover. It deserved a top grade, no question about it. Surely Miss Wannamaker would recognize my amazing ability and my destiny . . . to become a famous writer. She might even wonder—as she read and graded the stories in the privacy of her home—where in the world such a creative plot could have sprung.

"Dear class," she began as usual. "Today we shall begin by reading our stories aloud."

I felt faint.

FIVE

Miss Wannamaker's eyes skimmed over the desks. For a moment, they stopped at mine. I held my breath. This was it, the end of life as I knew it. Someone sneezed behind me. She looked up, and miraculously called on Andie. I could breathe again.

Andie went to the front of the room. She opened her folder and began. "Once upon a year—"

I heard no more. If Andie picked me to read next, there was only about five minutes between now and a living nightmare! The similarities between my main characters and the boy they loved were too obvious. Could I change the story, making it up as I go? Or become too sick to read?

My face burned with embarrassment as I thought how Jared would feel if I exposed our love to the whole world. Jared Wilkins—my first love. I couldn't risk it. Not to mention Andie's fury when she discovered *she* was in my story, too.

The class applauded. Andie had done a quick job of it last night. At least she didn't get hung from the ceiling by Miss W.

I'd rather hang than read, I thought as Andie's eyes penetrated me. I quickly put my head down, avoiding her stare like a firing squad victim.

Then I heard her say, "Jared Wilkins, you're next."

A truer best friend, I could never have, I thought as butterflies played tag in my stomach. I listened intently as Jared read his story. It was unique and well-written. About a mad scientist who met Einstein in a dream every night for seven days, and at the end, became not only sane, but wealthy from the secrets passed to him from the old genius himself.

Jared's story impressed me. We had more in common than I thought. I made a mental note to ask him about his writing ambitions.

The applause was loud; some boys whistled. Miss W frowned.

Jared's eyes scanned the classroom. He caught mine off guard. "I choose Holly Meredith," he announced. A declaration to the world! Under any other circumstances, I would have been thrilled with his words. But now they felt like a punch in the stomach.

I stumbled to the front of the class. How could I have concocted a stupid story like "Loves Times

38

Two"? I prayed for a miracle. If God could roll back the Red Sea for the Israelites, he could easily get me out of this mess.

I stated my title. Girls giggled; boys slouched.

"Excuse me, Holly, you'll have to speak up, please," Miss W said.

I smiled weakly.

Seconds from now I would reveal my first true love to the world, create more conflict with Andie, and maybe even lose Jared.

I was well into the second paragraph of my emotion-packed composition when the school secretary tiptoed in. All heads turned toward the door.

"The principal would like to speak with several of the students," she said politely.

Several turned out to be seven—all boys. Jared was one of them. This was it . . . my miracle! Jared would miss my true confession.

After the boys shuffled out, I continued reading with as little expression as possible, sneaking glances at Andie, hoping she wasn't paying attention.

Afterwards, we passed our stories to the front. Miss W mentioned tomorrow's grammar quiz. And that was that.

I tried to dodge Andie in the hallway, but she caught up with me. I braced myself for the onslaught.

"What's up?" she asked.

"Not much." I smiled. Who cared if Andie creamed me? At least Jared hadn't heard the story.

"What are you so happy about?" she persisted.

"Let's just say God answers prayer."

"I know *that*. What else?"

I changed the subject. "Hey, looks like you got your story written without my help."

"I was up till midnight doing what you could've done in minutes." We waved at Marcia Greene, the brainiest girl in our class, as she passed us in the hall. Andie continued, "That was some fantasy you read today. It doesn't have anything to do with Jared and the two of us, does it?"

"We writers get inspiration from many sources."

"But did you have to describe me down to my toenails?"

"Hey, I do my best writing when it comes to things I know—" this in my most sophisticated voice.

"Don't you mean *people* you know?" She was accumulating ammunition. "Aren't you worried Jared will hear about it?"

"Who's going to tell him?" I said. "Besides, it's already obvious how he feels about me."

"Is that so?" She had that familiar glint in her eyes.

We came to our lockers. "Look!" Andie said. There was a note, all squashed up, stuck in her combination lock.

I peeked over the top of her. "Who's it from?"

She opened it. "It's from Jared!" she crowed. "He wants me to practice his audition music with him after school tomorrow. At *his* house."

This was bad news. No, horrendous.

"He's heard I'm a piano whiz, no doubt," she bragged.

I opened my locker. No love notes for me.

"Want to tag along tomorrow?"

"No, thanks," I mumbled. "I promised Mom I'd watch Carrie tomorrow after school."

"Holly." Andie's tone had changed. She sounded hurt. "Can't we be as close as we were *before* we laid eyes on Jared Wilkins?"

I looked at her. She gazed back with pleading, puppy-dog eyes. I shook my head. "One of us has to back away from Jared," I said. "That's what we wrote in the Loyalty Papers: 'If we both like the same boy, one of us will give him up for the sake of our enduring friendship.' Can you give Jared up for the sake of our friendship?" I felt a giant lump in my throat. I didn't want to lose our friendship. But I didn't want to lose Jared either.

Andie grimaced. "It's time to revise those papers again."

"Why?" I asked.

"Might save our friendship—don't you think?"

The seriousness in her voice convinced me. "Okay," I agreed. "Saturday morning. My house."

Luckily the route to my next class took me past the principal's office. I was dying to know what had happened to the guys who were pulled out of Miss W's class.

I rounded the corner to the principal's office. Three ghost-faced kids sat waiting for the principal . . . remnants of my English class miracle.

41

I spotted Tom Sly. "What's this about?" I whispered.

"Someone saw them smoking behind the gym at lunch," he said.

My heart sank. But I defended him. "Jared? Smoking? He wouldn't do that."

"Grow up, girl. Jared's no saint. Besides, lots of good kids smoke." He pulled me over against the wall. "Listen," he said in my ear, "can you keep a secret?"

"You can trust me," I said. But could I trust him? After all, he had tried to resuscitate me for no reason.

"*I* was the one who caught them smoking." He snickered.

"Who else saw them?" I asked.

"You're looking at him."

"Did Jared see you spying?"

"No way."

"You're sure it was all of them?"

"Positive."

"When was all this going on?"

"Hey, don't grill me," he said. "During lunch. About 12:15."

The principal opened the door of his office and out came a tall, muscular boy. It was Billy Hill.

"There's one of Jared's smoking buddies now," Tom said.

"Billy Hill doesn't smoke." I watched him head down the hall, his shoulders slumped. He was one of the best players on the basketball team, and even though he wasn't a Christian, he was one of

42

the nicest guys I knew. "Billy looks so helpless," I said as he disappeared from sight.

"Not as helpless as you looked after you passed out."

I glared down at Tom, who was inches shorter than I.

"Your lips were so soft. We oughta try it again," Tom said.

Now he was admitting it! I gave him a dirty look. "You're disgusting."

"I was your hero!" he taunted.

"Jared was the *real gentleman*, dragging your face away from me."

"You can do much better than Jared Wilkins," he said cracking his knuckles one after another. "Like me, for instance."

"Don't get weird. We're barely even semi-friends." I tossed my head.

"I think you're gorgeous," he said.

Oh great, I thought, *not the class show-off*.

He must've seen me frown, because he blurted out, "Is it true what Miss Neff calls you in gym?"

I got away as fast as I could, but I still heard him calling after me, "Holly-bones, Holly-bones—"

The nickname stung all the way home. Still, that was nothing compared to the news about Jared. I couldn't wait to tell Andie—even if she *was* my rival.

I tramped up the snowy steps leading to my house. The porch swing swayed as I bumped past it. Daddy and I used to spend summer nights singing our hearts out on that swing. Sometimes

Mom came out to join us, surprising us with iced tea to sip on between songs. That was light years ago.

Carrie met me at the door. "I got an A on my math paper," she announced, waving it at me. A happy face smiled across the top.

"Great!" I congratulated her. "How about a snack?" I needed to get Carrie out of my hair so I could talk to Andie.

Once Carrie was safely settled at the table with an apple, I retreated to the downstairs bathroom with the phone. I dialed Andie's number. Mrs. Martinez answered. No, Andie wasn't home yet. She was still at her piano lesson. "Please tell Andie to call back as soon as she gets home," I said.

I hung up and paced the house, waiting for Andie's call. Finally I flopped in front of the TV beside Carrie.

"Where's Mom?" Carrie asked, snuggling with the cat. Goofey cleaned his paws.

"She said she'd be late from work tonight." I threw an afghan over our legs. "I hope she gets home soon. I'm hungry." Actually, I wasn't super hungry. I just didn't like it when Mom wasn't home. I guess I worry too much. When she's gone longer than I expect, my brain kicks in with dumb things like *What would happen to Carrie and me if something happened to Mom?*

Finally we heard the garage door rumble open. We raced to the windows and rubbed holes in the frost to peek out. Mom was home! Carrie and I raced through the kitchen to greet her.

44

"What do my darlings want for supper?" Mom asked as we hugged.

"I got your homemade pizzas out. How's that?" I said.

"Sounds wonderful." She removed her shoes on the way upstairs. "I'll make a salad in a minute." Mom looked worn out.

"*I'll* make the salad," I called up to her. She didn't answer. I hurried to preheat the oven. Then I pulled out a head of lettuce and began to shred it.

Carrie dropped a stack of letters on the bar. "Here's the mail."

I moved the mail to the desk in the corner of the kitchen. A blue envelope slipped out of the pile, landing on my foot.

I picked it up. My heart leaped as I saw my name written in bold black script. Who could it be? The handwriting wasn't familiar.

I checked out the return address. There was no name, just a street address and state. California? The last I'd heard, Daddy lived out there. My heart began to pound.

The phone rang. I grabbed it off the desk.

"You called?" It was Andie.

"Yes, and it's real important, but I'm stuck in the kitchen now, so I'll call you after supper."

"Can't you tell me quick?"

"I can't talk now."

"Just give me a little hint," Andie begged.

"It's about Jared and—" I looked up to see Mom on her way downstairs. "I promise I'll call back later."

45

Quickly I hung up. Excited and nervous all at once, I hid the letter in my pocket. Should I tell Mom? I would read it right after supper, then decide.

A letter from Daddy! This was headline news. Compared to *this*, the info about Jared was "Dear Abby."

SIX

"The pizza looks terrific," Mom said, sitting down. I had drawn the curtains across the bay windows, and the dining room light threw a warm yellow glow across the oak table. The heat vent behind me blew warm air at my feet. Now that Mom was back, it felt like home.

We bowed our heads as Mom prayed over the food. Goofey rubbed against my leg under the table.

"Long day?" I asked after the amen. She had pulled her hair back into a ponytail and scrubbed her face clean of makeup. Her eyes looked tired.

"Let's talk about your day, Holly-Heart."

"Well, to start with, you'll never guess what happened in English."

"Try me," she said, biting into a slice of pizza.

"I was reading my story about two girls in love with the same guy, when—"

"Now, Holly," she interrupted. "What kind of things are you writing for school assignments?"

"It's okay, Mom," I assured her. I could see this wasn't the time to share my English Class Miracle with her.

Carrie began to talk about her math test, and I knew our conversation was over. I picked black olives off my pizza, trying not to think about the envelope poking into my leg. I didn't want to tell her about the letter. Not now! Daddy was the last person on earth Mom would want to hear from tonight.

"I saw your principal's wife at the post office this afternoon," Mom said, helping herself to another piece. "Was there some trouble at your school today?"

"Kind of." I wondered how much she knew.

"Please choose your friends wisely," she said. It was a definite warning.

"My friends are okay, really."

Carrie piped up. "Whose night is it to clear the table?"

"Yours." I pointed to her. "I made the salad."

"*I* set the table," she hollered.

"Girls, girls, please," Mom said. "Supper was wonderful, Holly-Heart. Do you mind if I go upstairs and rest?"

"Go ahead, Mom. Carrie and I will clean up the mess."

"We'll talk later tonight," she said, leaving the room.

Carrie and I cleared off the table and stacked the plates in the dishwasher. I wiped the crumbs from the counter and picked the gooey pieces of cheese from the oven rack. Meanwhile the letter burned in my pocket.

As soon as we finished I headed for my room. Closing the door behind me, I pulled the letter from my pocket.

I crossed over to my windowseat and perched there, holding the letter in my hands. What would it say? Staring at the unfamiliar handwriting, I realized I wasn't ready to open it.

I hadn't seen Daddy since I was eight. I never knew what went wrong between him and Mom, and she never told me. She probably thought I was too young. All I knew is that one day he had gone away, and after a few months, even his cards and phone calls stopped.

Soon after the divorce we started going to church. That's when Mom became a Christian. And then Carrie and I accepted Jesus, too. I couldn't remember seeing Mom happier. She was excited about her faith, reading the Bible and talking to the Lord. Our new friends at the church helped us put our lives back together.

Now, after four years without Daddy, my world was comfortable again. Safe. Somehow, I had learned to adjust. Praying helped. I honestly believed my prayers would help bring Daddy to Jesus. Wherever he was.

I held the letter. A window to another world. Did I dare open it? I hesitated. No, it was safer the way things were, with Mom and Carrie and me on our own. I started to rip it up. Then I stopped.

Curiosity won out. I tore open the blue envelope and pulled out a handwritten letter.

I could almost hear Daddy's voice as I read.

Dear Holly,

Perhaps you don't remember me very well. You must be quite a young lady by now. I would like to get to know you and your sister again. How do you feel about that?

I realize it's been a very long time since you've heard from me. If you find that you are interested in getting better acquainted, perhaps you could come visit me during your spring break. I have remarried, and my wife's name is Saundra, and she has a son named Tyler. They would also love to meet you. Take your time in deciding this. My address is on the front of the envelope if you want to write.

I am sorry to tell you some sad news about your Aunt Marla. She is very sick with cancer. I know she is one of your favorite aunts, and since she is my only sister, I wanted you to hear about this from me.

I love both my girls. That may be hard for you to believe. But it is true. I would enjoy hearing from you.

Love,
Daddy

I stared at the letter. It seemed like forever since we'd sat on the porch swing, singing into the night. And the books. He'd read tons of them out loud to Carrie and me. At bedtime, after supper, on Sunday afternoons. Tears stung my eyes as I stuffed the letter, blue envelope and all, into my pocket.

I tiptoed to Mom's bedroom, gently touching the door. Silently, it glided open. I peeked in, hoping she was awake. Mom was sprawled out on the bed. I crept inside and pulled the comforter over her. *She'll be asleep for a while*, I thought as I wandered downstairs.

Carrie was sprawled on the floor in the family room, drawing lines in a dot-to-dot book. She was surrounded by crayons, markers, and a stack of coloring books.

"Carrie, this place is a disaster." I grabbed a handful of Crayolas. "Can't you keep these in the box?"

She ignored me. "Is Mommy asleep?" She played with the red bobble on top of her head. Her blonde fountain of hair gleamed in the lamplight.

"She's having a nap." I picked up a coloring book and started flipping through it.

"She's tired a lot."

"That's because she works all day with lawyers doing important work for their clients."

"But why is she so sad?" She looked up at me.

"I don't know." I wondered if Mom had heard about Aunt Marla. Maybe Grandma Meredith had called her. We were still close to Daddy's parents in spite of the divorce. Grandma and Grandpa never got used to it. I remembered hearing Grandpa say, "Why is our son leaving his perfectly wonderful family?"

Guess we weren't that wonderful, I thought. Anyway, they still thought of Mom as their daughter. And Carrie and I would always be their granddaughters no matter what.

The phone rang. I ran up to the kitchen to get it.

"Hey, Heartless," Andie said. "How come you didn't call?"

"I forgot." I turned my back to the family room and kept my voice low. "Something really major just happened."

"What?"

"It's my dad. I got a letter from him."

"Really? Wow! What did he say?"

I told her all about the letter, how Mom and Carrie didn't know about it yet, and how he wanted to see me again. I even told her about Aunt Marla.

"That's really sad—big time."

I swallowed the lump in my throat. "Yeah, I know."

There was a short silence. Then I changed the subject.

"Did you hear why those guys got called out of class today?" I asked. "Tom says he caught them smoking behind the gym during lunch." I felt strange spreading this kind of news around, but I wanted to see if Andie would defend Jared the way I did.

"That's wild," she said. "And hard to believe."

"I think it's some bizarre mistake."

"There's one way to track it down." She sounded like a super sleuth. "Let's corner Tom at his locker tomorrow first thing, since he seems to know so much about it."

"Okay," I agreed. I wasn't so sure I wanted to talk to Tom Sly again, but with Andie around he'd never dare call me names.

After I hung up, I pulled the blue envelope out of my pocket and folded it neatly. I went back down to the family room and curled up on my favorite spot on the sofa.

"What's on TV?" I asked Carrie.

Her eyes were glazed over. It was a commercial about breakfast cereal.

"Huh?" she whispered. I could see that the jazzy advertisement had won out over her dot-to-dot book.

"Never mind," I murmured, reaching for my red spiral containing every possible question on tomorrow's grammar test.

But I couldn't study. Instead, I daydreamed about the contents of Daddy's letter. I held the letter in my hand. It was strange reading his words, seeing his handwriting.

"What's that?" Carrie asked. The commercial was over.

"Oh, this?" I smoothed the wrinkles out of the California letter. "It's a letter from—" Fast thinking required.

"Who?"

"From someone you really don't know." It was

53

the truth. "I have to study now," I said, tucking the letter into my notebook.

"Hi, again," Mom announced, breezing into the room. She was dressed in her coziest pink robe and her elephant slippers. "Let's talk, honeys," she said, fluffing the couch pillows.

"Turn off the TV," I told Carrie.

"Come sit on my lap," Mom said to her. Goofey jumped on her lap too. Mom leaned over and gave me a hug. "I've been thinking about someone very special lately," she began. "Do you remember Aunt Marla and Uncle Jack? And the stairstep cousins?"

I nodded. How could we forget the Christmas we spent in Pennsylvania two years ago? We'd chopped down a nine-foot giant of a tree. The tip of it bent under the lofty farmhouse ceiling. Our stairstep cousins—we called them that because each kid was a little older than the next—Carrie, Mom, and I took half the day to decorate the monstrous tree. It was great fun for all of us, except Daddy wasn't there.

"Your Aunt Marla is very sick," Mom said softly.

"What's wrong with her?" Carrie asked.

"She hasn't been well for several months," Mom said, moving Carrie to the other side of her soft lap. "She has cancer. I've just heard from Grandma that some tests show that Aunt Marla might not have long to live."

"I know," I whispered.

Mom peered at me curiously.

"Would you be surprised if I told you Daddy wrote to tell me about her?" I stared down at my hands, then up at her.

"Not too surprised," she responded. But her eyes said differently. "Grandma told me that this news has changed your father."

I watched her face. "What do you mean?"

"Sometimes, when people learn that someone close to them is dying, it changes the way they view life."

"How?" Carrie asked.

"It makes them think more about how *they* want to live."

"I feel sorry for Uncle Jack and my cousins," I said.

"Let's pray that the Lord will give them extra strength during this painful time," Mom said.

We joined hands in prayer for Aunt Marla, Uncle Jack, and my stairstep cousins—Stan, Phil, Mark, and Stephanie. I prayed, too, that this lousy disease would disappear. Slowly, tears trickled down my face. Dear Aunt Marla's illness, and Daddy's letter—all in the same day—had caught up with me.

Mom wiped away my tears and looked into my eyes. "Do you want to talk?"

"I feel sad about Aunt Marla. And . . ." I drew a deep breath. "Do you think I'll ever be able to forgive Daddy for leaving?"

"That troubles you, doesn't it, honey?"

I nodded.

"It takes a simple, honest prayer of forgiveness,

and remembering each day that Jesus does the same for us when we hurt him," she said, taking my hand in hers and squeezing it gently.

"I used to miss him a lot." I looked away. "Then, when we didn't hear from him anymore, I figured he was gone forever. And now . . ."

"I know, honey." She leaned her head against me. "I know."

"You can read the letter," I offered hesitantly. It seemed like the right thing, letting her see it.

"Maybe another time," she said, her voice sounding stronger.

"Is it okay with you if I write back?"

"Of course. He's your father, Holly—that won't change. If you have a relationship with him, it's because you both want it."

Carrie had been listening to us silently, her eyes wide. "So *that's* the letter you were hiding."

Mom intervened. "Maybe Holly will share it with you some other time."

"Did I get a letter too?" She sounded hurt.

"No," I said. "But he says he wants to get to know you, too. I bet if you write him, he'll write back."

"Will Daddy start writing letters to Mommy?" she asked.

Mom said something that was probably pretty tough. "Carrie, love, your Daddy is married to another lady now. He has a new family."

Carrie never understood all this divorce stuff. *Who does?* I thought sadly.

"Does he have some new kids?" she asked.

"He has a stepson."

"Will Daddy ever come visit us again?" Carrie asked.

"If you see him, most likely it will be at his house," Mom said.

I couldn't believe she offered that. So I sucked in some air and dropped an enormous idea on her. "Dad says he hopes you'll let me fly out to visit him during spring vacation."

Mom sat motionless. "I'll have to think about *that*." She pulled us against her "Now, don't we have homework tonight?"

While Mom coached Carrie with math flash-cards, I tried to study for tomorrow's test. But all I could think about was Daddy. Did I really want to see him again?

My notes on adverbs blurred, so I set aside my English notebook. Other things seemed more important than maintaining my "B+" average. Right now anyway.

A few hours later I was propped up in bed, reading my devotional book without the usual suggestion from Mom. Bearie-O stared straight ahead as I tucked the blue envelope inside my Bible, marking the verse for the day. It was Psalm 46:1. "God is our refuge and strength, an ever-present help in trouble." How did the writers of my devotional always seem to know the perfect verses to choose?

I slipped under my blanket and turned out the lamp beside my bed. Bearie-O fell forward, his face pressed against my lavender comforter. I leaned my elbow against his love-scarred head.

A timid breeze caressed the aspen trees outside my window. Through the window I could see the shadowy form of their bare branches. But try as I might, I couldn't see Daddy's face, his tall frame, or those gentle blue eyes in my imagination. Only the outdated picture on the nightstand came into view, faint in the twilight.

SEVEN

"Ready for action?" I asked.

Andie nodded. We stood in the hallway before our first class, plotting our strategy. We had vowed to corner Tom and make him talk—whether he wanted to or not.

Andie grabbed my arm and we marched down the school hallway, on our way to the stakeout.

"Super sleuths to the rescue!" I said.

We giggled.

"Got any spy glasses?" Andie said, peering around, her eyes squinting.

"Here." I handed her an imaginary pair, and she put them on with a flourish.

"Shh, there he is." Andie pointed. Tom had just finished unlocking his locker and was taking off his coat. "Remember, *I'll* handle this."

We strolled over and stood silently on either side of him. He slammed his locker shut and turned around. He looked surprised to see us, but he covered it quickly.

"Hello, beauties," he said, eyeing both of us. "How may I assist you today?"

"There's something we need to ask you," Andie said. "We figured you'd be the one to approach about this, since you know everything about everyone around here." She laid it on thick. Boys fall for her routine, and since it works, she keeps recycling her approach.

"Since you put it that way," he said, "I'd be happy to fill you in. *Both* of you," he said, with an endearing look at me.

He'd fallen for Andie's ridiculous line!

"So," she said, "What were you doing spying on Jared?"

That's it, Andie, get straight to the point, I thought.

"Who wants to know?" he said, getting defensive.

"Let's put it this way. It's important," Andie said.

"What do you care?" he asked.

Andie was smart enough not to tell him we were crazy about Jared. Or that we hoped to clear his name.

"He attends our church, and we thought—"

"You thought he was a good church boy, huh?" he jeered. "Well, *nobody's* perfect."

"Christian kids should know better," I chimed

60

in. "We have a perfect example to follow. God's son."

"Oh, really?" he mocked.

Andie pressed on. "What were you doing behind the gym during lunch yesterday? I thought I saw you inside watching intramurals."

"Well, you were wrong."

She turned to me. "Holly, you saw him there, right?"

Come to think of it, I had! He *had* been inside the gym the whole hour! I nodded.

"So, maybe you didn't see Jared and those guys smoking at all. Right?"

"Back off. You don't know what you're saying," Tom hissed.

Bingo! Andie, the genius, had touched a nerve.

Tom didn't look like he was going to give away any secrets about Jared's behavior. But he *did* look guilty. Now I was beginning to suspect something.

"Guess we'll have to get our information from a *reliable* source," Andie said.

"Excuse me, I have a class to catch." He shoved past us. We looked at each other and grinned knowingly.

"He's hiding something," Andie said, watching as he disappeared into a crowd of kids.

"Definitely," I agreed. "Meet me at lunch?"

"Okay." And we were off to first period.

The morning dragged by. I could barely pay attention in history and math. The whole situation with Daddy and Jared weighed on my mind. I caught myself daydreaming several times.

When lunch time came, I was eating a roast beef sandwich as Andie came into the cafeteria, carrying her lunch tray piled high.

"Look at this," she said, balancing her tray on the back of a chair. "Jared gave me some of his leftovers. He said something about having time-tests in gym. Guess he didn't want to be too stuffed with food."

"The coach really puts the guys through the ropes on those tests," I said, remembering what I'd heard about them last year. I slid a piece of lettuce out of my sandwich.

Andie handed over a dish of apple cobbler. "Here, this is for you, from Jared."

"Jared?" I picked up my spoon. My cheeks burned.

"You're blushing," she sang.

He was thinking of me! Still, I worried. "Is this because he thinks I'm too skinny?" I asked.

"Think? Anybody can *see* that. But don't worry. Things'll change soon." She took a bite of her sandwich. "I can't wait till after school. Are you sure you can't come over to Jared's house with me for the audition practice?"

I shook my head. I didn't want Andie to know, but I didn't like being around her and Jared at the same time. So I said, "I promised Mom I'd be home on time to be with Carrie."

On the way out of the cafeteria I ran into Jared. His eyes lit up, and he fell into step with me. My knees felt like jelly. Again. But all I could think of was how to bring up the subject of what had happened yesterday.

"Good luck on your time-tests," I said.

"Hey, thanks. Did you get the dessert I gave to Andie?"

"Sure did."

"Hope you didn't mind."

"I wasn't sure why you gave it to me."

"What do you mean?"

"I'm self-conscious about being thin." I looked away, embarrassed.

"Holly, I think you're *perfect*. Besides, I like tall, thin girls."

Good! That left Andie out. She was only four-feet-ten and on the chunky side.

"Are you ready to wow them at the choir auditions?" he asked, waving at Marcia Greene as she passed us in the hallway.

"I will be by the end of the week. Mom's going to accompany me." I hoped he'd say that Andie was accompanying him, but he didn't. Maybe it was no big deal to him.

"Did you hear the choir's going to Southern California?"

My heart jumped. That's where Daddy lived!

"Tough competition too," he said. "Half the youth group is trying out, and there's only room for thirty."

"Guess we better practice," I said. But my mind wasn't on the auditions. I wanted to know the truth about what had happened yesterday behind the gym. We stopped in front of the entrance to the boys' locker room. If I was going to ask, I'd better do it now.

I took a deep breath, "Were you really smoking at the noon hour yesterday?"

"No way!" he said. "It was a complete set-up. I was having lunch with my dad—you can't have a better alibi than that. Someone's trying to get me booted off the team, and I know who."

I thought I knew who it was too. *Tom Sly.* "I bet he's threatened by the competition," I said, "and he doesn't want to share the accolades with some new kid."

"Right," he agreed. "Where did you get the vocabulary?"

"From books," I said, realizing I was going to be late for home ec. "I devour them."

"Hey, I like that. By the way, I heard you wrote some terrific story for the assignment in English."

"I liked yours a lot. Ever think about becoming a writer?" I couldn't believe how much fun he was to talk to.

"It's one of my life goals," he said. "Did you have someone in mind when you wrote your story?"

Who'd told him about "Love Times Two"? Surely not Andie. I played dumb. "What do you mean?"

"Maybe we can talk about it sometime," he said, moving towards the locker room. "See you later," he shouted over his shoulder, flashing a grin that melted my heart.

"Good luck on the time-test," I said.

"Thanks, I'll need it." He was about to push open the locker room door when he turned and said, "Holly, I'll call you tonight. How's eight o'clock?"

"Perfect," I said. I waved and took off down the hall before he could see the huge grin on my face. I kept smiling all the way from my locker to the home ec room. I couldn't wait to tell Andie that Jared was cleared of the smoking charges. But the rest of our talk I was keeping to myself.

I got to class just in time. Hastily, I settled onto one of the work station stools just as Mrs. Bowen began giving instructions for today's culinary creation: lasagna. When she finished, Andie made a mad dash for the sink and started to scrub her hands vigorously.

"Hey," I said, "we're making lasagna, not performing surgery."

Andie looked serious. "Tom grabbed my arm in the hall. He's mad. Tried to get me to quit asking questions about Jared smoking. I'm scrubbing his contamination off me."

I laughed. "Jared's not guilty, just like I thought."

"*You* thought? We both knew it wasn't true. Did I miss some more important info?" She slipped a green and white terry cloth apron around her chubby waist.

"I just talked to Jared himself," I announced. "He's off the hook. His dad vouched for him. Besides, Jared says Tom's paranoid—thinks Jared will show him up on the team. Tom's been number one around here too long. Well, move over number one, here comes Jared Wilkins!"

The girls at the next station gawked.

"You're having a personality change," Andie said. "I've read about things like this. Love does strange things to people."

"My countenance shineth," I said. I pranced around, waiting for the noodle water to boil.

"She needs help," Andie said to the others. "Come along, dear." She led me back to the work station, pretending I was senile.

We fried up the ground beef and prepared the tomato sauce. After draining the noodles, we started creating the lasagna casserole layer by gooey layer.

"Whoops!" I almost spilled the tomato sauce.

"Watch what you're doing!" Andie warned.

My mind was on Jared—and on Daddy's letter. I still couldn't believe he had written to me and completely by-passed Mom. He'd overlooked the fact that she could veto the whole thing!

We put the lasagna in the oven and began to clean up. We were almost ready to take the lasagna out when a siren rang out in the distance. Because of all the ski slopes in the area, we were used to this sound. But *this* siren, instead of fading away as it climbed into the mountains, grew louder and louder. It sounded like it was heading for our school!

Andie raced to the window. "The ambulance is out front!" she said.

Mrs. Bowen came to the window, and soon we

66

were all there, squeezing in, trying to see. "Look, Holly!" Andie grabbed my arm. "I think that's Jared's mother!"

"Are you sure?" I asked.

"I saw her in church last week; I think that's Mrs. Wilkins." She stared at me, her face filled with fear.

"Something terrible's happened," I said.

Pressing my nose against the icy window, I saw a white stretcher emerge from the ambulance. Two men wheeled it into the gym entrance.

Minutes later, there was more commotion. Now the stretcher carried a tall, brown-headed boy wrapped in wool blankets.

It was Jared. *My Jared*. Was he alive? Mrs. Wilkins stepped inside the ambulance. The doors closed.

My heart sank as the siren sang its mournful song.

EIGHT

The ambulance was long gone when I stepped away from the window. Like a zombie, I wandered over to Andie. She had taken the lasagna from the oven and was staring at it sadly. The cheese was brown and some of the noodles were burned black around the edges.

"I feel sick," I said, holding my stomach.

"I can't believe Jared's been hurt!" Andie cried. "We have to find out what happened."

"Someone next period might know," I said. Silence fell as we surveyed the lasagna. "You want to take it home?" I asked.

She nodded. We wrapped the pan and put it in the refrigerator. Then we finished cleaning up.

"I'll probably bomb for sure on the English test next period," I said, twisting the dish towel.

Andie pushed the chairs under the tables. "Who cares about English tests—Jared's hurt!"

Tears blinded my eyes.

The bell rang as Andie put her arm around me. "Let's go to the restroom. We'll pray in there," she whispered.

I gathered up my books. Andie led the way to the bathroom. She always seemed stronger in situations like this, even when we were little girls. For me, the tears came all too quickly.

"C'mon, let's pray," Andie said, grabbing my hands. I balanced my books on the sink. Andie's prayer was long and fervent. When we opened our eyes she looked up at me, poised for action.

"Here's the deal," she said. "After school we split to my house and get Mom to drive us to the hospital."

"Okay," I said, "but I'll have to call my mom first."

A toilet flushed. The serene moment gushed away. An astonished girl came out of the stall. I guess she'd never heard anyone pray out loud. She turned to stare at us before making her departure. We smiled back.

"I feel better," I said.

"Me too," Andie said. We headed for English in silence.

Settling in for the test, I noticed Tom Sly and Billy Hill were missing. Phooey! No chance to ask them about Jared.

My stomach churned. I felt as prepared for this test as a computer without a printer. The short time I'd spent studying wasn't going to earn me the kind of grades I was used to getting.

The questions on the test blurred as I thought about Jared in the hospital.

Hospital. A scary thought. It reminded me of Aunt Marla. She was dying! My favorite aunt. It wasn't fair. She was so cool—always doing neat things for Carrie and me, spoiling us when we went to visit at Christmas and in the summer.

Just then, Marcia Greene, the smartest kid in class, brushed past me on her way to Miss Wannamaker's desk. She had finished the test! Daydreaming was a luxury I couldn't afford. I gripped my pencil and filled in some answers.

After class, Andie and I hung around until two boys were finished talking to Miss W. They'd been in gym during last period, so we headed for them like vultures.

"Hey, Jeff, do you know what happened to Jared Wilkins in gym?" Andie asked.

"Yeah," Jeff Kinney said. "He fell off the trampoline during warmups for time-tests."

"He was up really high," Mark Jones added.

"What happened?" I asked.

"He lost his balance and fell. It was gross. You could see the bone sticking out of his leg," Mark said.

"Will he have to have surgery?" I asked.

Mark shrugged. "Who knows?"

"Let's go," Andie said, pulling me away.

Mark called over to us, "Have you girls gone and lost it over Jared?"

"Mind your own business," I snapped. We turned and headed down the hallway.

Andie looked at me, surprised. "Aren't *we* getting sassy?"

"You haven't seen anything yet." I held my books against my chest. "Mark's attitude is really sick."

"You got that right."

"What does the entire school's male population have against Jared, anyhow?"

"You've seen how new kids are treated around here. We're a bunch of snobs," Andie said.

"But they're *jealous*, too. For once here's a guy who has more than muscles and good looks—he's smart, too."

Andie nodded, then gave me a fierce look. "I have a feeling Tom Sly knows something about Jared's accident." She jammed her books into her locker. "And I intend to find out what."

♥   ♥   ♥

At Andie's house, the smell of brownies pulled us into the kitchen. Mrs. Martinez looked just like Andie, with dark curly hair and sparkling eyes. "Brownies?" she asked.

We plopped down at the bar while Mrs. Martinez cut two large pieces.

"Mom, there's been an emergency at school," Andie blurted out. "Can you take us to the hospital?"

"What's wrong?" her mother asked, pouring a glass of milk.

71

I spoke up. "We want to go see Jared Wilkins. He's hurt."

"What happened?"

We explained the accident, and Mrs. Martinez listened sympathetically. But at the end she shook her head. "I think the two of you should stay put, and pray for him instead. I doubt you could see him now anyway," she said.

Andie's curly-haired twin brothers bounced into the kitchen. Seeing the treats, they tripped over each other to get to us.

"Me get tweet?" one of the two-year-olds asked.

"Yes, Donnie. You get treat," Andie said, pulling the pan of brownies closer. She cut each of them a small piece. They jammed the brownies in their mouths and went running around the kitchen. Mrs. Martinez followed them to make sure they wouldn't mess up things.

"Still on for tomorrow?" Andie asked.

"What?"

"The Loyalty Papers, remember?" Andie said. "We were going to revise them. And now that I see how much we both like Jared, I think it's urgent."

Andie's comment confused me. I thought things were improving between us.

Just then I remembered. "Andie, I forgot to call Mom! I better do that now." I made a dash for the kitchen phone and dialed the number of her office. She answered.

"Mom? I'm at Andie's house. I didn't go home

right away because there's been an accident . . . a friend of mine."

There was a silence, then Mom, sounding displeased, said, "Holly, your sister's been home alone all this time. Usually you're more responsible than this."

"But I *had* to come straight to Andie's house," I said, defending myself.

She didn't buy it. "You should've called. I'll phone Carrie to let her know you're on your way."

She hadn't even asked me about the accident! All she cared about was Carrie, who was perfectly able to take care of herself. Frustrated, I said, "I don't need a lecture about this, Mom. I really don't!" I hung up without saying good-bye.

When I arrived home, Carrie was watching a cartoon. "How was your test today?" she asked.

"Probably flunked it," I told her. "Where's Mom?"

"She's home now and real upset." The tone of her voice spelled trouble.

"Why?" I slouched into the arms of my favorite sofa.

"Something about your disrespectful back talk." Carrie was sounding like a grown-up.

"Guess I should go up and apologize," I complained. I stood and trudged up the stairs. Her bedroom door was closed.

I knocked and waited.

"Come in," she said.

Not daring to look at her, I plodded over to the bed and sat down. The first few seconds were tense. Then she put her arm around me. "I love you, Holly-Heart, you know that."

"Mom?"

"Yes, honey?"

"It's getting harder to be—" I didn't know how to tell her that I was feeling more and more rebellious. But, only sometimes. "To be—obedient."

She smiled knowingly. "There are hundreds of changes happening in your body right now. Your emotions will fluctuate, swing up and down. And most of the time, you won't understand why you're feeling the way you are."

"So this will happen more and more?"

"It's part of becoming a woman," she said.

I picked up the rose-colored potpourri pillow on her bed. Hugging it against my flat chest, I breathed in its sweet fragrance. "I was very sassy on the phone. I'm sorry, Mom."

"I forgive you, honey. We all have moments like that."

"Mom, you wouldn't believe what happened at school today—"

From then on it was like opening a can of soda. My words poured out. I could always talk to Mom. The fiery rebellion was gone.

After supper we got a call from the prayer chain. The actual facts: Jared was stable, but he was suffering some momentary amnesia from the blow to his head. As for his leg, it would be in traction until they operated. Then he'd be in a cast for a month or so.

So much for basketball this season, I thought. I was disappointed for him. And I was dying to see him.

"When can I visit him?" I asked Mom. I was washing pans, Carrie was drying, and Mom was putting away the leftovers.

"We'll have to call the hospital and see," Mom said.

Carrie teased, "Maybe his amnesia wiped *you* out of his memory forever."

"No chance!" I said, flicking her with soap suds. "I'm unforgettable!"

The phone rang. Mom answered. It was Grandma Meredith. Carrie and I looked at each other, then watched Mom anxiously. Her smile faded, and the lines in her forehead deepened as she listened. Finally she said, "I can't leave the girls, but I wish I could help in some way." She sat down slowly.

There was a long pause.

Mom leaned her blonde head against her hand. When she spoke, it was barely a whisper.

"Tell Jack and the children we're praying," she said. Then she hung the phone up hesitantly.

Carrie and I stood like statues as Mom searched for a tissue in her pocket. Neither of us dared to speak.

"Darlings," Mom began slowly, "Aunt Marla's not doing well. They think she has only a few weeks before—" Her voice broke.

We knew.

Later, we made an attempt to rehearse my

audition piece. Mom made tons of errors. Her heart wasn't in it.

In bed—hours later—I read out loud to Bearie-O. Having him close reminded me of the special friendship Andie and I enjoyed. But lately, things were so up and down between us.

I continued reading, but my concentration was wacky. Uncle Jack and the stairstep cousins—Stan, Phil, Mark, and Stephanie—kept creeping into the mystery novel I struggled to read. What would they do if Aunt Marla died? My mind wandered in and out of the story.

Daddy strolled across page twenty-five. What about an answer to the spring break question?

Jared called to me from chapter three. His leg had to be amputated.

In chapter four, Andie demanded a major rework of our Loyalty Papers.

Halfway through chapter five, Carrie threatened to cut off her hair. She was sick of my sarcastic remarks and didn't want to look like me anymore.

It was close to midnight when all of them finally faded away. And I fell into a restless sleep.

NINE

The next day, I slept till almost nine o'clock. Mom was relaxing with the paper when I wandered downstairs.

She glanced up. "Good morning, Holly-Heart. Ready for breakfast?"

"Definitely!" I was starving as usual. Mom fixed a platter full of pancakes with scrambled eggs on the side, then sat down to chat with me as I ate.

"Mom, can I make snickerdoodles after lunch?" I asked. "Andie's coming over. She wants to revise our Loyalty Papers, and I want her to be in a good mood."

"Are you going to bribe her?" Mom asked, her eyes twinkling.

"No." I decided to change the subject before she asked too many questions. "Where's Carrie?" I said, finishing off my last bite of eggs.

"Watching cartoons," Mom said. She sipped at her peppermint tea, her hands wrapped around the mug to warm them.

"Did she say anything about cutting her hair?"

A shocked expression crossed Mom's face. "Not that I know of. Why?"

"Just checking," I said, recalling the parade of problems dancing across the pages of my book last night. But the problem I cared about most was Jared. After we had finished cleaning the kitchen and Mom was safely out of the room, I dashed for the phone and called Andie.

"Hi." She sounded alert and ready for action.

"Whatcha' doing?"

"This is so cool, Holly. Listen—Jared's parents agreed to let me bring my keyboard to his hospital room."

"What for?" I guessed what she was up to.

"The choir director wants to audition him in the hospital."

There was a long silence while I groped for something to say. Andie had one-upped me, and I knew it.

"Sounds interesting," I said at last. That old green-eyed monster was poking its nose into my business again. "He must really want Jared in the choir."

"Good tenors are hard to find," she said.

"What about his amnesia?"

"He doesn't remember anything that happened yesterday."

"Nothing?" I thought about the phone call he'd promised. "What about the fall off the tramp?"

"Nope, not even that."

"How do you know all this stuff?" I asked.

"My mom and his mom talked."

Real sweet, I thought.

"When will you practice with him?" I asked. I was dying for her to ask me to go along.

"Tomorrow afternoon. He's supposed to rest during the morning. Which is probably a good idea. He's in traction, you know."

Her know-it-all attitude irritated me, but I said, "Still coming over today?"

"Yep. We've got major work to do on our Loyalty Papers, remember?"

Of course I remembered, but I secretly hoped that *she* had forgotten. "Are you sure you want to revise them?" I asked.

"Of course! Got 'em ready?"

"Sure," I said, giving in. "The Loyalty Papers await. And I'm making snickerdoodles after lunch. Wanna help?"

Andie said, "I'll help make them disappear!"

"Fabulous," I said. We hung up.

I worried about revising the Loyalty Papers. It might create a major argument, especially since Andie and I were both crazy over Jared.

Upstairs, I showered, then dressed in my jeans with frayed knees, and a blue plaid oversized shirt. Counting the days till my birthday was priority on my morning agenda. In giant numbers I wrote *22 days* on the scrap paper stuck to my bulletin board. It still seemed too far away to plan my big bash.

After lunch I mixed together some flour, cream of tartar, soda, and salt. Then I stirred in soft butter, sugar, and eggs. Andie arrived just as I began rolling the dough into walnut-sized balls.

"Mmm, yum!" she said, eyeing the cookie sheet.

"They'll be ready in eight minutes," I said. "Let's have some apple juice while we wait."

"Thanks," Andie said as I poured the cold juice.

I flicked the oven light on, and we watched the snickerdoodles do their thing—puffing up at first, then flattening out, leaving a crinkled top.

After they were done, I let them cool. Then, piling them high on a plate, we headed for my room.

"Ready to do some major revisions on the Loyalty Papers?" Andie asked, plopping down on a corner of my bed.

I was glad she couldn't see the face I made as I sorted through my dresser drawer, searching for the Loyalty Papers. There they were—in the legal document holder Mom had given us years ago. It was a reject from the law firm where she worked as a paralegal.

Andie set the plate of cookies in the middle of the bed and began shuffling through our papers. Absentmindedly, she reached for a snickerdoodle and ate it as she read. I sat on the opposite side of the bed and took one cookie, watching her face for any warning signs.

She frowned. "Look here," she said. "We really missed it on *this* paragraph." She pointed to the page, clearing her throat like the principal getting the kids' attention in assembly. "Page three, paragraph seven." She paused. "This is absurd, Holly."

"What is?" I peered down at the page between us.

"This dumb idea. It says that one of us has to back away from a boy if the other person likes him too."

"Well, we wrote that two years ago, before Jared ever happened to us. Maybe we should add something about whoever liked him *first* gets to keep him," I said.

"Oh, no, you don't. That won't work. Besides how could we know for sure who liked him first?" Andie flipped through the next two pages. "Were we so dumb to think we'd never attract the same boy?"

"Well, look at it this way," I said, trying to stay calm. "Since we're both so different—in looks, in personality, in the way we think—maybe we were on to something when we wrote that part."

"I'm sick of your logic," she said, standing up and brushing the crumbs all over my floor. "Call me when you're thinking clearly."

"Wait," I said. "What's wrong with my idea?"

Andie glared at me. "Don't be dense. Neither of us will back off." She headed for the door.

"Where are you going?" I asked.

"Home—to practice Jared's audition music. See you, Holly. Thanks for the snickerdoodles."

A lot of good the snickerdoodles did. I stared glumly at the plate. One lone cookie was left. I picked it up and ate it. Without licking my fingers, I shuffled the pages of our Loyalty Papers. Who cared if they got messy. They were useless now!

To get Andie and Jared off my mind, I joined Carrie for a few video cartoons. But nothing could stop me from thinking about Jared, lying all alone in the hospital.

After the videos, I grabbed Mom's attention by juggling four cookies at a time. When I quit showing off, the kitchen floor was a crumby mess. Goofey licked up the sweet crumbs.

"Something's troubling you, Holly," Mom said, handing the broom to me. "You're not yourself."

"It's Jared. No, it's Andie. She and I both like Jared. And now *everything's* crazy."

"Can't the three of you be friends?" she said so innocently I thought she was joking.

"It doesn't work that way, Mom."

"Well, enlighten me," she said, rinsing out a rag for me to wash the spots off the floor.

"Jared wants to ask me out, and Andie's freaked out over it." I looked up at her from all fours.

"Ask you out? Where are you going?"

"Nowhere, that's just what you call it when a guy likes a girl and doesn't want her to hang around with anyone else." I tossed the rag into the sink.

"I see," she said. But of course she didn't. The old days, when Mom was a teen, were long gone.

Later in the afternoon, Carrie and I tagged along with Mom while she went shopping. At the checkout, we bagged groceries for her, racing to see who could get the most food in each bag.

"Oops, this isn't working," Carrie said, trying to pick up one of her sacks. Two boxes of microwave popcorn tumbled out.

"Look out!" I cried, as two oranges found their freedom, rolling under the counter. The clerk gave Mom the grand total, and a strange look.

"Big mistake bringing *you* along," I said to Carrie, as I reached around the back of the counter, groping for the oranges. "*You* get them."

"Mom! Holly's being a pain," Carrie yelled.

Mom looked frazzled. "Please go out and wait in the car, Holly." She dangled the car keys in my face.

"Why don't you send Carrie?" I argued.

"She's too young. Now go," Mom said firmly.

"Perfect," I whispered.

Outside, in the cold car, I turned on the ignition. Grandpa Meredith had let me start his car last summer when they came to visit. I had backed it in and out of the driveway dozens of times.

Shivering, I turned on the heater full blast. The lights of the village twinkled as dusk approached. Mom had no right to send me out here. Pulling a tablet out of the glove compartment, I wrote: *Dear Daddy*. It was time for an answer to his invitation. I hid the half-written note in my coat pocket when I saw Mom and Carrie coming towards the car. *They don't need to know about this*, I thought, feeling sneaky good about my secret.

The following day was Sunday. I had trouble listening to the sermon. Andie sat across from us, next to her parents. Her brunette hair, perfectly in place, framed her round face. I imagined her playing the piano for Jared, their eyes catching secret snatches of unspoken adoration. It was unbearable, so I blocked it out.

I underlined the minister's text in my Bible with a red pen. Carrie cozied up to mom in the pew. I wished I were somewhere else. Somewhere like Dressel Hills Hospital, in traction with Jared.

There was only one reason why Andie hadn't asked me to go with her to Jared's audition. No doubt in my mind. She wanted all his attention! Some best friend she'd turned out to be.

Carrie peeked around Mom and flashed a less than angelic grin. Her missing teeth completed the impish look.

Most of the time I loved Carrie, but sometimes Mom spoiled her rotten. Getting away from her for a full week during spring vacation was a fabulous thought. If I got to go to California to visit Daddy, I'd leave Andie behind too. The only person I would miss was Jared.

At home, Sunday dinner tasted blah. Usually I can't get enough baked chicken and onions, but Jared was on my mind and in my heart.

After the dishes were stacked in the dishwasher,

Mom grabbed a notepad and sat at the table. "Let's plan your birthday party, Holly-Heart."

I glanced at the calendar. "It's too far away."

"The days are flying by," she said, clicking the pen. "How many friends do you want to invite?"

I paused to count. "I can think of at least ten."

"I was thinking more in terms of seven. Including you, that's eight. An even number."

"I can add. Besides who cares about even numbers?"

"Maybe we can plan this later." Mom sounded exasperated. I didn't blame her; I was giving her a tough time on purpose.

"Just forget this year. Maybe turning fourteen will be better than this." I stormed out of the kitchen, certain that Andie was doing her musical thing right now at the hospital with Jared. More than anything, I wanted to be there.

Upstairs, I curled up in my window seat and wrote the rest of my letter to Daddy. I tried to imagine what his new life was like. This, after all, was *his* house. He and Mom had fallen in love with Colorado. They'd moved from Pennsylvania after they got married, making a life together in this skier's paradise. And what a skier Daddy was! He even gave me skiing lessons, starting when I was five. After a few practice runs, it was like breathing. Daddy said I was a natural.

Surely his new life wasn't half as good as it was with us. And what about this new stepson of his? Somewhere out there I had a nine-year-old stepbrother.

A knock on the door interrupted my thoughts. Mom poked her head in the door. "Holly-Heart, your friend Andrea's on the phone."

My heart skipped a beat. *News about Jared!*

"I'll get it here," I hollered down the hall, louder than usual. I reached for the hall phone.

"Hello?"

"Hey, Heartless, still speaking to me?"

"Why shouldn't I be? *You* were the one who stormed out of here yesterday."

"Jared had his audition."

"How was it?"

"Jared's voice is as fine as he is."

"I *know* that. How's Jared *feeling*?"

"Feeling? Well, uh, I know you won't believe this, but we held hands today, when no one was watching. Is that what you mean?"

"I don't believe you."

"Well, do you want proof?"

"You have to be lying," I said.

"Hang on, I'll get Jared to tell you himself."

"You're disgusting, Andie," I yelled. "And you call yourself my best friend? I'm tearing up the Loyalty Papers. It looks like they don't mean anything to you anymore."

"Holly, what's going on?" she said, acting innocent.

"You're ruining my life."

"What's happened to you? You've changed so much. Honestly, I thought you'd be happy for me." She poured it on like honey and vinegar.

"You want me to congratulate you for taking my boyfriend away?" I yanked at my shoe strings.

"But you never really had him."

"This is truly the end of our friendship," I said, kicking my tennis shoes down the hall.

"You'll change your mind if you want to be on choir tour."

"What's that supposed to mean?"

"The director told us—Jared and me—about the theme for the tour. It's unity. 'Our hearts in one accord,' Mr. Keller said. You know—getting along. Doesn't allow fighting over boyfriends or anything else."

I'd had it with her preaching. "If *you* don't make it into the choir, getting along will be the easiest thing in the world," I said, hardly believing how sarcastic my words sounded. Or how easy it was to say them.

"I'm in," she announced with great pride.

"How do you know?" I said. "Auditions aren't until Tuesday."

"Mr. Keller wants *me* no matter what. If there are too many sopranos, he'll use me at the piano." Downright haughty, that's how she sounded. "Uh, excuse me, Holly. Jared is calling me. They're bringing a tray up from the cafeteria for me. I've got a dinner date with Jared. Bye."

Andie's words stung me. Stumbling to my room, I fell into bed and stared at the underside of my canopy, feeling cheated. My best friend had trespassed on *my* territory. *On my heart.*

87

T E N

I don't know how long I stared like that, but soon I had the urge to grab Bearie-O and throw him across the room. I didn't need him reminding me of Andie.

Mom called me downstairs to play caroms. I played even though I didn't feel like it.

"Please, will you take me to see Jared?" I begged when Carrie's turn came around.

Mom placed the white shooter on the board, aimed, and shot. "I don't know the family very well."

"You could get to know Mrs. Wilkins," I said as two of my green caroms slid into a side pocket. "Please?"

It took three more turns and saying "please" at least five more times before Mom finally gave in.

She agreed to take me to the hospital right before the evening service at church.

Dressel Hills Hospital was small, but well decorated. Cozy mauve couches and chairs were scattered around the waiting area. Potted palms and spider plants gave it a comfortable feeling. Oil paintings of local spots—mountains, waterfalls, and meadows—were spotlighted on the wall.

Mom asked for Jared's room number at the receptionist's desk. We walked down a long, narrow hall. I became more nervous with every step. What would I say to Jared? Would Andie still be there?

We rounded a corner, and I spotted Mrs. Wilkins chatting with Andie's mother in the waiting area near room 204—Jared's. So Andie *was* here. Mom shot me a glance. I nodded and pointed back at her. I wanted *her* to make the introductions.

Somehow I managed to smile and shake hands with Mrs. Wilkins, a small woman with blue eyes and a smile just like Jared's. "Why don't you go on in and see Jared?" she said. "Andie's with him."

"Are you sure it's all right?" I asked.

"Well, to tell the truth, he might already be sleeping," Mrs. Wilkins said. "He just had some morphine for the pain."

Jared in pain? My heart jumped. I wandered over to his room.

Pausing at the doorway, I spied Andie. She sat

curled up in a chair, close to Jared's hospital bed, like she was monitoring his every breath. He was propped up with a zillion pillows, his right leg supported by a pulley system above the bed.

Andie looked up. "Holly!" she said in her most charming voice. "Come right in!"

I approached the bed just as Jared let out a tiny high-pitched snort. He was snoring!

Andie explained, "He's had morphine for pain."

"That's what his mother said." I found another chair and pulled it over next to Andie's and sat down. A long silence fell. I was boiling inside.

I couldn't hold it in any longer. "Look, Andie," I said. "Jared likes *me*, I know he does."

She crossed her chubby little legs. "Maybe he did once, but this is *now*," she said. "It's over . . . you're history."

This was beyond my worst nightmare! Jared interested in Andie? He had said he liked tall, skinny girls.

"I know you're wrong," I argued. "You must have been dreaming when you thought he was holding your hand."

"Do you want a written statement?" She leaned closer to Jared, her eyes scanning the rings and pulleys that held his fractured leg in place. "He wants me to watch over him while he sleeps."

"Oh, pl-e-ase." I rolled my eyes and snorted. "He doesn't need mothering, Andie." Then I lit into her. "You're the poorest excuse I know for a best friend."

"What about you? You didn't back away when you knew how much I liked him, did you?"

"That's different," I managed to say. "He was the first boy to accept me as I am."

"You mean skin and bones?"

A low blow! Something snapped inside. "That's it," I shouted. "You'll never see our Loyalty Papers again."

"Liar, you don't know what you're saying." She fluffed her dark locks. "You can't handle life without me."

"I'd like to try," I growled. "Why don't *you* go home and leave me alone with Jared?"

"If I'm not here when he wakes up—well, I just don't know what he'd do. We have a very special bond," she said in her sickening-sweet voice.

"Well, he must be desperate, then. Why don't you just pack up your precious keyboard and get out of here?"

Mom and Mrs. Wilkins peeked their heads in the doorway. Mom looked puzzled. "Is everything all right in here?"

"Not really," I said. "Make her leave."

"Girls, can you solve your problems elsewhere?" Mom asked. She motioned for me. I got up reluctantly and went to her.

Jared woke up. "I–I heard voices," he said.

Andie jumped up to reassure him. "It was nothing."

Mr. Wilkins came in, carrying a white styrofoam cup brimming with hot coffee. He was good-looking too, with blond hair and a mustache. He pulled a chair over next to the bed.

"Nice of you girls to come see our boy," he said.

"Girls?" Jared said sleepily. "Where?"

Mom's firm touch on my arm signaled the end of my visit. "Nice to meet you," she said to Jared's parents. "We'll be sure to mention Jared during the prayer requests at the service tonight."

We smiled and shook hands all around, then we headed down the hall. Carrie held Mom's hand, and I moped behind. I felt like fighting. With Andie, with Mom—with anyone in sight.

"What's come over you?" Mom asked as we drove home in the snowy stillness.

I shrugged.

"Holly?" she said in her warning voice, which meant, *You'd better talk to me—or else.*

"Don't you remember?" I said. "It's all part of becoming a young woman. Isn't that what you said?"

"Holly, I've never seen you so rude. What's the matter?"

"For as long as I live, I never want to see Andrea Martinez again," I announced as we pulled into our driveway.

A strange sense of delight swept over me as I slammed the car door and stomped into the house. Like an arrow, I darted straight to my room. There I pulled the Loyalty Papers from the special folder. I looked at them for a moment, then I ripped each page in half and scattered the pieces all over the floor. Finally, I slam-dunked Bearie-O into the trash can, head first.

This was it. Our friendship was *over.*

ELEVEN

Tuesday afternoon—choir auditions! To sing with a traveling group had always been one of my dreams. But as I sat waiting in the hallway leading to the choir room, I wasn't so sure my dream would come true. The place was crammed with teens. They lined the hallway. They leaned against the plaque-covered wall. They sat cross-legged on the floor. Each reviewed last-minute dynamics and phrasing.

Mom and I waited together. She sat calmly, waiting for my audition. I twisted my hair.

"We've practiced over twenty times," I told Alissa Morgan, the girl ahead of me.

"Good idea by the looks of things." She stood on her tiptoes, searching for someone.

"Are all these kids in the teen group?" I asked.

"Sure are." She spotted her friend and called, "Hey, Danny, over here."

A tan-faced boy with reddish hair bounded over to us.

"How's it going in there?" Alissa motioned toward the choir room.

"It's fierce competition," Danny Myers said. "How are *you* doing? Nervous?" He touched her hand.

"I'll be glad when it's over," she said.

"Relax, you'll make it." Then, spying me, he said, "I remember you. Holly Meredith, right?"

I nodded.

"Your mom makes the best cookies ever. Snickersomething."

I smiled. "Close. Snickerdoodles, and they're *my* favorite, too."

"She brought some to our Christmas bake sale. That's when I first met you and your sister. You two look so much alike."

"The tall and the short of it," I replied.

"How tall are you, anyway?" Alissa asked.

"Almost five-eight." I beamed down at her.

Danny grinned. "One more inch and you'll catch me." He had a comfortable way about him.

"Wanna grab some pop before you go back in?" he asked Alissa.

"My throat *is* dry," she said. Danny took her hand and led her down the hall.

I sighed inside. *Some day, a boy will treat me like that.*

Thirty minutes dragged by. There was a heaviness in the air. One girl came out of the choir room in tears. Next came a boy, smiling. He jumped up and down all the way to the end of the hallway, exclaiming, "Yes, yes!"

"*He's* confident," Mom said, looking up from her novel.

An older girl poked her head out the choir room. "Holly Meredith, you're next."

With as much courage as possible, I entered the choir room. I did fine on the sightsinging and my prepared piece . . . but the arpeggios. Gulp!

On the way home, Mom chattered with excitement. "You sang like an angel, Holly-Heart."

Maybe she thought so, but I knew better.

"Tuesday—An Alto's Nightmare," I wrote the heading in my journal. "I survived it," was the only mention I made of the pitiful audition. The rest of the diary entry was taken up with how sweetly Danny Myers treated Alissa Morgan. I couldn't remember seeing them together before. But it's no surprise since I wasn't going to youth meetings yet.

It felt weird going this long without talking to Andie. I pulled Bearie-O out of the trash and told *him* all about my audition. He was a good listener. Never talked back. Never threw junk out of his locker, making piles in the hall. Never stole boyfriends. Or called me stupid nicknames, like Heartless. Even though he really belonged to Andie, after six years I thought of him as mine.

Wednesday morning arrived. Eighteen days to thrilling thirteen! I wrote the number on my bulletin board. The days were crawling by like snails.

Before mom left for work, I asked her about my party. "Can we plan it tonight?"

"After school."

"Perfect!" I said, twisting my hair.

"You'll split your ends," Mom said.

I wanted to say *who cares?* but bit my tongue instead.

That afternoon, following gym class, Andie bragged about Jared's musical genius to the girls in the locker room. The only good thing about gym today was Miss Neff didn't call me "Holly-Bones." It was a first. *Maybe she noticed some development that I missed*, I thought, standing sideways at the mirror.

My hair was still damp from a quick shower when I reached for my history book and slammed my locker. Racing towards history class, I accidentally bumped into Danny Myers.

"Oh, excuse, me," I said as he picked up my books.

"No problem," he said. "Holly Meredith, right? Five-eight? Look-a-like little sis? Bookworm mother, right? Favorite cookie—snickerdoodles?"

"You're a walking, breathing computer chip, right?"

He stopped, took a long look at me, and smiled. "That's my specialty—memory. I work at it."

I straightened my books. "It shows."

"See you at youth service next Tuesday?"

"When I'm thirteen. About a month to go."

"Really?" There was that smile. "They should change those rules." And he was off in the opposite direction.

For a microsecond I forgot about Jared Wilkins.

In history class I doodled on my notebook. How long before my letter arrived at Dad's? I'd mailed it on the way to school this morning. Mom was still in the dark about what I'd decided.

The teacher droned on about the decisive battle in the Norman conquest of England. I day-dreamed. I could catch up by reading it tonight.

After history, I caught up with Billy Hill heading for his locker. "Wait up," I called.

"Hi, Holly," he said.

"Any news about Jared?"

"He had his surgery Monday night. They put a rod in his tibia bone."

"Which one's that?"

He pointed to his own leg. "Shinbone."

"Is he in a cast yet?"

"Yep." He ran his hand through his hair.

"For how long?"

"About six weeks. Bummer, huh?"

"So, he'll get it off by spring break?"

He scratched his head. "Yeah, it should be off by then." He looked serious. "The worst part about this whole thing is it shouldn't have hap-pened."

"What do you mean?"

"Several guys were spotting Jared on the tramp. One of them was Tom Sly. When he saw Jared falling, he backed away."

I couldn't believe it.

"Who knows," he added. "Maybe Tom was looking for a chance like that. They'd been hassling each other a lot during practice games after school."

"Really?" I said. "Do you think Tom wanted to hurt Jared?"

"It was hostile-city between them. You heard about the smoking thing Tom tried to pull on Jared and me, didn't you?"

I nodded. "That was so weird."

I stopped with Billy at his locker. There was a note taped to the outside. "Looks like a note from the coach," he said.

I looked over his shoulder as he read it. "Late practice?"

"Yeah. Things are tough without Jared around."

"Looks like Tom's revenge is messing things up for the team."

"You bet it is." He closed his locker. "You like Jared, don't you?" He looked me square in the eyes.

I felt feel my cheeks getting hot.

"You're blushing," he said, with a smile.

"Gotta run," I said, heading for my next class.

In English, I jotted down seven names on a notepad. These kids were getting invitations to my thirteenth birthday bash. Andie wasn't on the list. Jared was.

TWELVE

I slammed the back door behind me and dropped my bag of books on the bar in the kitchen. *Home, sweet home,* I thought.

"Holly?" Carrie yelled from the family room.

"What?" I shouted back, unzipping my coat.

"Jaredsomebody called."

My hand froze at my zipper. Jared! My heart pounded. I went to the top of the stairs and tried to sound casual. "When?"

Carrie skipped up the stairway and watched as I hung my coat in the hall closet. "He called right after school," she said. "He wants you to call him back."

"Okay, thanks for taking the message." I picked up my book bag. Slowly, I headed toward the steps leading to the bedrooms, then raced to the phone in Mom's room, so Carrie wouldn't see me. Or hear.

"Room 204, please," I told the hospital operator. Butterflies flittered in my stomach as I waited.

"Wilkins' Torture Chamber," a voice said.

"Is that you, Jared?"

"Who else?" he said, laughing.

"It's Holly."

"I'd know your voice anywhere." He paused. "How's school?"

"Okay, I guess. The team misses you. Everyone does," I said, thinking I was the one who missed him most. "I visited you Sunday afternoon, but you were snoring."

He chuckled. "Morphine knocked me out a couple days before surgery. Doc says I'm going home tomorrow."

"Really?" I was dying to see him again.

"How'd your audition go?"

"Let's just say I've sung better."

"Hope you make it." His voice was soft. "Choir tour wouldn't be the same without *you*, Holly-Heart."

My heart flip-flopped. "Mr. Keller's going to post the list this weekend. Lucky for you, you already know you made it." I folded my long hair over the top of my head. It hung down like a satiny curtain in front of me. "I might be going to visit my Dad in California for spring break," I said.

"You can't do that . . . It's the choir tour."

"But isn't it this *summer*?"

"It's during spring break, and we're going to Disneyland."

"Guess I'll have to visit my dad another time," I said, wondering how I could've been so mixed up.

Jared changed the subject. "Don't we have a skiing date this weekend?"

"With your leg in a cast?" Some comedian.

"And why not?" Jared asked, flirting. "No, really," he said, more seriously. "I'll be home from the hospital on Friday, and the youth group's going tobogganing Saturday at Jake's Run. How 'bout going along to keep me company at the lodge?"

Jake's Run!—the steepest, wildest toboggan ride this side of the Continental Divide. It had a cozy, A-frame lodge with a coffee shop and a lounge with a huge stone fireplace. "How can you get around—with your cast?" I asked.

"Oh, I've got crutches now. And my folks think it would be good for me to get out, as long as I'm careful. What do you say?"

As much as I wanted to go out with Jared, Mom would never let me date now. She always said I had to be much older, and oozing with responsibility before I could think of dating. Besides, I wasn't old enough to go on the youth group activities yet. I sighed. "I don't think I can," I said.

"Why not?"

I dodged the question. "Isn't Andie going to be there?" I asked. I still had doubts about Jared, and they confused me. What had really happened between Jared and Andie at the hospital? Had she lied about holding hands with him?

"I don't know," he said. "Why?"

"I thought you liked Andie. *She* thinks you do."

"No chance," he protested. "Andie and I are just friends."

Carrie suddenly stood in front of me. She tugged at my shirt, even though I shooed her away. Her eyes were demanding little specks growing wider with every second.

"Look, I've gotta run, my little sister needs me."

"I'll call you tomorrow then," Jared said. "Bye."

I held the phone in my hand, reluctant to hang up. Turning to Carrie, I said, "Please don't do that ever again. This call was private."

"So that's why you came up here to talk." Her childishness bugged me. "You're hiding from me."

"You'll understand some day."

"Are you in love?"

"You'll never know." I raced her to the kitchen, where we helped ourselves to carrots and dip.

If this was love, why did I feel so happy and so miserable all at the same time?

The next two days in school dragged on and on. Jared called me Thursday night and pestered me about going to Jake's Run with him. I told him I hadn't asked my mom yet.

Finally it was Saturday. Sleep in! Mom jostled me out of my covers. "Wake up, Holly-Heart. This is the day we've been waiting for. The choir list will be posted at church soon." She tossed Bearie-O at me.

I flipped my leg over the side of the bed. Slowly easing out, I stood and stared at the mirror. Was this the face of a traveling singer?

After breakfast the phone rang. It was Andie.

"I'm not sure I want to talk to you," I said.

"Listen, something's really crazy," she said. "It's just too awful."

"Why are you calling me?"

"Well, I know we're not talking—"

"No kidding," I interrupted, wondering what was so important.

"It's such a shame," she said. "It really is."

"*What* is?" I asked.

"Holly, I'll try to break this to you gently."

"Break what to me?"

"You asked for it," she said. "Your name's nowhere to be seen on the list for choir."

I slammed down the phone. Enough of her gloating. Mr. Keller and his precious choir could go sing in their sleep for all I cared.

Determined to ignore Andie and her nasty news, I marched to the garage. There, I found a box of lawn and leaf trash bags. I scribbled a note to Andie, pinned it to Bearie-O and stuffed him inside.

"I'm going out, Mom." I yanked my coat and gloves out of the closet.

"Where are you going in this cold?" she called.

I slung the trash bag over my shoulder. "For a walk. I'll be right back."

I trudged down the sidewalk where Andie and I had played the don't-step-on-a-crack-or-you'll-break-your-mother's back game when we were kids. It was only a few blocks to Andie's house. When I arrived, I noticed the mail carrier coming up the street. Perfect! In a few minutes the deed would be done.

I hid behind a clump of aspen trees in front of her house till the mail truck passed by. In a flash, I dashed to Andie's mailbox, opened it, and shoved the trash bag inside—Bearie-O and all.

Later, when I arrived home, I told Mom to forget about going to the church.

"Why, honey?" she said, looking up from the dining room table, where she was writing a list.

I tossed my mittens up onto the shelf in the hall closet. "I already know I wasn't picked for choir. But it's okay—I didn't want to see Andie's fat little face every day during spring break anyway."

"What's going on between the two of you?" Mom asked.

"We're through—done. The final end of us has come." Then I made the cold announcement about Daddy. "Oh, by the way, thought you'd like to know—I've decided to visit Daddy during spring vacation."

She looked surprised. "Isn't this a bit sudden?"

"I'm sick of being around here. I'm sick of everything!" I sat down on the floor in a heap.

"Holly-Heart, you're terribly upset about the

104

choir tour, aren't you?" She left her list behind and sat on the floor beside me, stroking my hair.

"It's that, and everything else. You don't understand anymore."

"Maybe we could talk about it."

"It's too late. My letter to Daddy has probably arrived by now."

"We could've discussed it, don't you think?"

"Daddy must think I'm old enough to decide where I want to spend my vacations."

I got up and trudged upstairs. At the top, I turned to see Mom, still sitting on the floor, looking sad.

In my room, I tried to think of five creative ways to ask Mom about going tobogganing with the youth group. But when I came down to talk to her, the only thing I came up with was, "Can I go to Jake's Run with the youth group this afternoon?"

She was sitting at the dining room table cutting out coupons. She looked up, scissors in hand. "It's a little short notice, don't you think?" *Snip* went her scissors.

"I guess, but I just found out about it," I said as politely as a charm school graduate.

She added three more coupons to her pile. "From whom?"

Somehow I knew *that* was coming.

"Jared Wilkins," I said.

"Didn't he just get out of the hospital?" There was no fooling her.

I pleaded my case. "Yes, but he needs some company and some fresh air."

"He wouldn't be foolish enough to go tobogganing with his leg in a cast, would he?"

"Oh, Mom. Be fair. We won't be outside. We can talk inside the lodge."

"That's too exclusive. Besides, the whole idea of going with the group, is to be *with* the group."

"But I've been alone with him before. We went to the Soda Straw and—"

Oops. Whatever made me say that? Mom's eyes got all squinty and she said, slowly and evenly, "You did *what*?"

"We just had a Coke one day after school, and Andie came by anyway, so it wasn't that bad. I'm responsible. Please, Mom? Please may I go?"

"No," she said flatly. "Not this time, Holly-Heart."

"Don't call me that," I yelled over my shoulder. That nickname meant I was loved, but I certainly didn't feel like it, at least not by her.

I stomped up the steps, thinking of ways to escape for the afternoon. Five minutes alone in my room and I had it. When Mom was ready to go grocery shopping, I'd say I had unfinished homework. Then when the house was empty I'd hop a bus to the church. Perfect!

After lunch, I volunteered to clean up the kitchen. Mom was impressed, Carrie relieved.

By the time Mom was ready to do the shopping, I had convinced her to let me stay home to do a report for school. She fell for it.

House empty, I slipped into my soft pink turtleneck sweater and brushed my hair. My heart pounded with the daring adventure ahead—my first real date with Jared!

♥　　♥　　♥

The lodge above Jake's Run buzzed with noise as skiers clumped in their boots across the wooden floor to the snack bar. Jackets hung on pegs, their bright colors splashed against the dark paneling.

Jared and I went through the snack bar to a quieter spot, a small room with cozy sofas and tall windows overlooking the slopes. A roaring fire crackled in a white brick fireplace nearby. I warmed my feet as Jared showed off his storytelling abilities to the perfect audience. Me.

"That's fabulous," I said. "You should write these down."

"Sometimes I do. But mostly they're in my head. How about you?"

"I'd write all the time, if I could."

"I think we're made for each other," he said. "What do you think?"

I laughed, soaking up the attention. "What . . . just because we both write?"

"That's one of the things I like about you, Holly. You don't play games. You're honest."

He wouldn't have said that had he known I'd lied to get out of the house.

Later, I signed his cast. In red letters, I wrote, LOVE, HOLLY. Our hands touched.

"Does this mean we're going out?" he asked, propping a pillow under his bad leg.

I ignored the question. "Here, let me help you."

"Well, Holly-Heart?" I was surprised he used my nickname again.

I blushed. "Okay," I said.

Jared's eyes twinkled. "Fabulous," he said softly, using *my* word.

We played six games of checkers while the youth group tobogganed. If it hadn't been Jared smiling and flirting across the checker board at me, I would have been miserable. The sun's rays disappeared behind the mountains as supper time approached. By now, Mom would know the truth.

All the way home Jared held my hand. He said I was perfect. Tall and skinny . . . so what?

I believed him. This was first love at its best. Well, almost. The guilt from lying and sneaking off grew more powerful as each snow-packed mile crunched under our bus.

On the last mountain pass, our bus broke down. Danny and Alissa and several others got out as the driver surveyed the problem. I watched Alissa from inside the bus. She looked like a snow princess; her face glowed—half windburn, part sunburn—and a little adoration for Danny thrown in.

I checked my watch. Mom would be worried to death by now. Jared winked at me and my heart flip-flopped.

Three hours and a growling stomach later, I turned my house key in the lock. Carrie caught me tiptoeing in. "Mom, she's home," she shouted, throwing her arms around me.

Mom glanced up from the sofa in the living room and began folding the newspaper in half. She stood up slowly. Her precise movements spelled trouble. "You've been gone a long time, Holly-Heart." It was a statement, not a question.

She knew.

"I won't lie to you anymore, Mom. I went with the youth group to Jake's Run."

She squinted her eyes. "It was deceitful, Holly, and willfully disobedient. You're grounded. No friends, no TV, and no phone for a week."

"A week?" I cried.

"There's leftovers in the fridge. Eat something before you go to bed. I'll have a list of chores on the table in the morning."

"But, Mom, I—"

"No back talk or I'll add more." She turned towards the kitchen. I'd never seen Mom this rattled before.

"She forgets how it feels to be a kid." I let the words softly slip from my lips.

"I'm gonna tell," Carrie said.

"Who cares?" I shot back, taking the steps two at a time.

Safe in my room, I wrote a heading for today's journal entry—"A Secret Date with Jared Wilkins." Paying for my deceit with a week's grounding was even trade for the hours I'd spent with him.

THIRTEEN

The first week of February—seven days of pure boredom! Going to school was what I lived for. Jared was back, and I was his faithful helper—carrying his tray at lunch, sharpening pencils in class, and helping with his crutches in the hall and everywhere else. Andie acted angry, following us around. Jared was polite about it even though it was obvious she couldn't accept the facts. Jared was mine now.

After-school hours dragged endlessly. Even Bearie-O was unavailable for trouble-dumping. And when Corky showed up on my porch on Tuesday with a note pinned to his ear, I knew my friendship with Andie was in deep trouble. But I didn't care. I had Jared.

Finally, the week was over. Freedom! Talking on

the phone was pure heaven. Best of all, my birthday was getting closer. Mom stocked up on four flavors of ice cream for the birthday bash. One of the flavors was bubble gum, with delicious mounds of pink gum scattered in. And ten toppings! I couldn't wait for the best ice-cream party ever. On Sunday afternoon I did fancy cuttings with lavender and blue crepe paper. Everything was set for my party the following Saturday.

Then on the Thursday before my birthday I came home to find a note propped against the cookie jar. *Holly, Carrie and I are at the travel agency. We'll be back soon. Love, Mom.*

I poured a tall glass of milk, stirred chocolate syrup in, and grabbed two cookies to nibble. My imagination ran wild.

Great, I thought. *She's planning some exotic travel adventure during spring break while I'm out in California visiting Daddy.*

While pigging out on cookies, I wrote a love note to Jared. The first letter to my first love. I was half finished when the garage door rumbled open. Quickly, I hid the perfumed stationery.

Carrie ran into the kitchen out of breath. "We got tickets and Mom has something to tell you."

Was it Switzerland or the Orient?

Mom walked in at a snail's pace; her face looked drawn. She pulled up a kitchen chair. Sat down. I didn't want to look at her. *This is some cruel trick*, I thought. *Did she really think I'd cancel my plans to go with them instead?*

111

"Holly-Heart." She breathed a heavy sigh. "Aunt Marla died this morning."

I was stunned.

"We're flying to Pennsylvania tomorrow."

Carrie asked, "Do we have to wear black to the funeral?"

"No, darling," Mom said, pulling her close.

Tears trickled down my cheeks.

"Her pain is finally over,," she said, holding out her arms to me. "She's with Jesus now."

"What about Holly's party?" Carrie asked, rubbing her eyes.

"I'm sorry, dear, we'll have to postpone it," she said, picking up Goofey and stroking him.

I twisted my hair. "Who feels like celebrating, anyway? I'll call everyone."

I hadn't even begun to anticipate the possibility of this happening. The timing was terrible.

Grandpa and Grandma Meredith met us with hugs and tears at the airport. They drove us through the narrow tree-lined streets to their house. Quietly unpacking, I thought back to the happiest times in this house. When Mom and Daddy were still married, we used to come for week-long visits in the summer. Uncle Jack and Aunt Marla and our cousins would drive the short distance to Grandpa's house on the Fourth of July. We kids would make short order of the corn on the cob until Grandpa teased that we might turn into walking ears of corn ourselves. At dusk, we'd write our names in the air with the sparklers Uncle Jack gave us. Daddy and his sister, Aunt Marla, would kiss and hug goodbye.

I swallowed hard, fighting back the tears. Those days were forever past, not just because Aunt Marla was gone, but because Daddy was, too.

Carrie came in and sat on the quilted bedspread. "Mommy says our dad will be at the service tomorrow. Do you think he'll bring his new wife and kid?" Carrie asked.

"Maybe," I said, brushing her hair. "I wonder if he'll recognize us." I felt giddy with excitement and sadness all mixed together.

"We sent school pictures to him last fall."

I stopped brushing. "Oh, yeah, and mine looked pathetic because I couldn't get my hair to do anything." I looked in the mirror. My bangs looked droopy now, too. It was the humidity. Even in the winter, Pennsylvania air was heavy with moisture. I sprayed more hair spray on them.

The funeral was on Saturday—the day I was supposed to have my ice-cream party. The foyer of the church was crowded when we arrived. People lined up to sign a formal-looking white book on a small table encircled with red roses. Mothers with young children and their executive-type husbands—probably men who worked with Uncle Jack—waited to say their goodbyes to Aunt Marla.

The family was supposed to gather in a small reception room behind the sanctuary. Carrie and I followed Mom down the long hallway to the private room. Grandma and Grandpa sat with

Uncle Jack and the cousins. We sat in soft chairs behind them.

Relatives I hardly knew stood around. Mom introduced Carrie and me to them; they were from Daddy's side of the family.

Behind me I heard whispering and turned to see who it was. In the doorway stood a handsome man wearing a navy blue suit. He was holding hands with a smartly dressed woman.

Four years of mounting curiosity hit me in the face. The man was my father.

"Holly?" he said. "What a beauty you are." He turned to the woman. "Honey, I want you to meet my daughter, Holly."

"Hello," I said, suddenly shy. I reached out to touch her gloved hand.

"Holly, I'd like you to meet Saundra, my wife."

By then Carrie was tugging at me to leave. I grabbed her arm and turned her around.

"Well, hello there, Carrie," Daddy said.

She looked up at me, confused. "That's him?" she whispered back at me.

Daddy smiled. "So nice to see both of you."

Saundra said, "We were happy to receive your letter, Holly."

"Yes," Daddy said. "I was planning to call you to set up the flight schedule. But now we can discuss it in person." He stepped towards me like he wanted to hug me, so I gave him a quick one.

"I'll see you at the family dinner tonight," I said, turning to look for Carrie.

She was standing across the room beside our

cousin Stephanie who sat, eyes swollen, leaning against Mom. It was time to go to Aunt Marla's funeral.

The church was filled with a sweet fragrance from the many floral sprays. The organ played softly, and voices were hushed. I touched the tissues in my dress pocket. I knew I'd need them.

After the funeral, we waited to ride in one of the black limousines to the cemetery. Carrie begged Mom to let Stephie ride with us.

"Uncle Jack wants all of the children to ride together," Mom said as we walked down the church steps.

The limo pulled up. There was only room for two more.

"I'll ride in the next one," I said. Mom nodded.

Another limo came around and I got in. Daddy and his new wife climbed in behind me. He looked lousy; his face was pale and his eyes were red.

I felt numb. Aunt Marla's funeral wasn't exactly the place to meet my long-lost Daddy.

The ride to the cemetery was awkward. Here I sat across from this Saundra person trying to be polite when I really wanted to shout: Leave me alone with my father!

What was she doing here anyway? She probably had never met Aunt Marla. Then, to top things off, she began chattering about spring break!

"We've planned a delightful time for you," she said. "It's next month, isn't it?" She opened her purse, took out lipstick and a mirror, and began to touch up her already bright red mouth.

"The last week in March." I glanced at Daddy. "Maybe you should talk to Mom about it."

"Tonight will be plenty time for it," he said, adjusting his striped tie. He was as handsome as I'd remembered. "Tomorrow is your birthday," he commented. "When are you flying back?"

"We'll get home late tomorrow night." Too late to have the ice cream party. Too late to celebrate my important birthday with my friends. With Jared.

Saundra asked, "Is there something special you'd like?"

I twisted my hair as I thought of the most special things in all the world. They couldn't be purchased by her or anyone. But there was *something*. "The latest mystery by Marty Leigh is out. That would be nice."

Saundra smiled, closing her compact mirror with a click. Did she really think she could make points with me that easily?

"How are you doing in school?" Daddy asked. "Good grades? Lots of friends?"

I told him about my B+ average. I didn't tell him about my writing, or about Jared, my first love.

That night at supper, Stephie sat with Carrie and me. Her nose was red from too much blowing, but her eyes looked less swollen. When the caterer came around to get our beverage orders, Stephie ordered pop, then looked at her dad to see if he would disapprove. Uncle Jack didn't say anything. His usual fun-loving smile was gone.

"Mom would never let me drink pop at meals," Stephie whispered to us. "Things are going to be different without her."

I nearly choked on my ice water. I couldn't imagine being eight years old and motherless.

"Things changed at our house when Daddy left, but not that much," Carrie said. I wondered if she really remembered.

After the lemon angel food cake was served for dessert, Grandpa signaled for everyone's attention. "My granddaughter Holly will be celebrating her thirteenth birthday tomorrow. Please join me in singing the birthday song."

He motioned for me to stand while they sang. Relatives I'd never met and friends of Uncle Jack's sang happy birthday with gusto. I glanced at Daddy. He winked. Mom, at the other end of the long table, beamed with pride. Some birthday party! I should have been eating ice cream with Jared right now.

Then I felt ashamed. Aunt Marla was gone, and all I could think about was missing Jared.

Late that night, lying awake in Grandpa's big house, I stared at the shadows dancing eerily on the ceiling. In a few minutes I'd be a teenager. "Dear Lord," I prayed. "Let this be my magical night." He knew what I meant.

The next morning I woke with a jolt. A small backbone pressed against me. It was Carrie's.

I lay still in the quiet. The clock's ticking soothed me. Today was Valentine's Day. *My* day.

Uncle Jack and the cousins came for breakfast. The boys wolfed down their pancakes.

"Slow down, fellas," Uncle Jack said. Usually he would have made a joke of the boys gobbling them down.

I remembered why we'd called them the stair-step cousins. Sitting across from them was like looking at a descending scale. Stan first, then Phil and Mark. And Stephanie last.

Grandpa came downstairs, carrying a box wrapped in bright pink and red paper. He planted a wet kiss on my cheek. "Happy birthday, Holly-Heart."

Inside, a huge white teddy bear stared up at me. Grandma had cross-stitched a red heart on him, and a ten-dollar bill shaped like a bow tie was pinned under his chin.

"Thank you." I hugged the bear first, then Grandpa and Grandma.

"What's his name?" Stephie asked.

"I'll have to think about it first. Let's see what his personality's like." I pulled out my chair for Grandpa. "How did you know what I wanted?"

"A little bird flew around and chirped it in this ear." He pulled on his left ear.

"Oh, Grandpa," Carrie said. "You're just teasing."

The doorbell rang. Grandma hurried to the living room.

"Happy birthday, Holly." It was Daddy—and his wife.

"Come in," I said shyly, inching towards them.

Daddy pulled an envelope out of his pocket. It was a gift certificate to a national chain of bookstores. "You can get that mystery book you wanted and many more," he said with a grin.

"You should be able to buy a month's worth," Saundra said, smiling too broadly.

"Thanks, I love it." The words choked in my throat.

Carrie lost interest and disappeared upstairs with the cousins. Mom hadn't ventured into the living room. I could see her alone in the kitchen clearing things away.

"We really can't stay," Daddy said. "We have to catch a plane, but we'll be in touch."

Uncle Jack held out his hand. "Good to see you again."

Daddy ignored his hand, hugging him instead. "Take care of those kids, Jack," he said, a twinge of longing in his voice.

Grandma kissed him and said to call when they got home.

"Take it easy, Son," Grandpa said. His eyes glistened.

"I'll send you a ticket soon," Daddy said to me. I reached for him. He held me. And they were gone.

FOURTEEN

After Daddy left, we went to church—all but Uncle Jack. He said he needed some time alone. I wanted to say something to make him feel better, but there was nothing to say. So as we headed out the door, I ran up and hugged him hard. He hugged me back and kissed me on the forehead.

We sat in the back of the church. During the service we passed tissues up and down the row. Even the joyful songs seemed terribly sad. I hardly heard the minister. But I kept praying, *Dear God, be with Uncle Jack and my cousins. Please help them to be all right.*

After church I retreated to the room where I'd slept. Silently, I closed the door. It was time to pour out my feelings on paper. Rummaging through the suitcase, I found my journal. In honor of my dear Aunt Marla, I wrote her birthdate and death date in my diary. I stared at it till the tears came. She was too young to die—just two years older than Mom!

The flight home was long and boring. When we got back, Mom set the suitcases on the kitchen floor and promptly marched Carrie off to bed. I went up to my room and read my Bible until my eyes drooped. They felt like Bearie-O's looked. I missed his droopy eyes and his owner, my best friend. But I didn't miss Andie's disgusting attention-getting routines.

I hugged my new birthday bear to me and thought of Jared. It had been three whole days since I'd seen him—the longest we'd been apart. I couldn't wait to see him again. Turning thirteen was perfect with him in my life!

The next day at school I told everyone on the list about the *new* date for the party: Saturday, February 20. Everyone but Jared. I couldn't find him. Not in the library. Not at his locker between classes.

At last, I saw him in the cafeteria at lunch . . . with Andie! She was getting grated cheese for his spaghetti. I waited in the hot line, seething, as she slid in next to him to shake the cheese on his plate.

I wanted to hang her upside down by her fat little toes.

Billy Hill slipped in line behind me. "Looks like Andie's earning points with your boyfriend," he said. "The minute you left for Pennsylvania, she moved in."

"She did?" I was crushed.

"Yeah, she didn't waste one minute," he said. "Flirting, helping him with his crutches . . . you name it."

"That little . . ." What word could describe her? Or him? They looked too cozy over there—talking and laughing. I set my tray down on the table and seethed.

Billy looked at me. "You okay?"

I blew my breath out hard. "Jared's a two-timing jerk, after all."

"Funny. Andie doesn't seem to mind," Billy said.

I sat down with my spaghetti. "How could he do this to me?" I said between bites.

Danny and Alissa came in together. They sat at the end of our table. Before they ate, they bowed their heads.

"Weird," Billy mumbled, getting up to leave. "See you around, Holly. Hang in there."

To get my mind off Jared, I moved over near Danny and Alissa. They smiled and said hi. "Ready for choir tour?" I asked them. I had decided that even if I couldn't go on the tour, I wouldn't sulk about it.

"Sort of, except Alissa can't go," Danny said.

Alissa explained, "We're moving next week."

"Really?" I said. "How come?"

"My dad got transferred to another state," she said. She and Danny stared sadly at each other.

While we talked, I watched Andie talk and flirt with Jared, twisting her curls around her fingers.

Worst of all, he was flirting back. Once I even saw him reach over and ruffle her hair playfully.

When I finished my dessert, I excused myself and headed to my locker. Inside, I was seething with anger. At myself for trusting Jared. At Andie for moving in on *my* territory.

Andie came careening around the corner. "Look out!" she screeched, dropping a load of books on the floor in front of her locker.

"Watch where you throw things," I said, sidestepping her hefty stack.

"These are Jared's and mine *together*." She huffed and puffed and opened her locker.

"Where's Jared now?" I asked.

"Waiting for me on the steps," she said, pointing down the hall.

"You just couldn't stay away from him, could you?" I snapped. "I'm gone for a couple of days, and—"

"We're starting where we left off in the hospital, before *you* messed things up. Jared said so."

"He's totally insane," I mumbled into my locker.

"That was dumb what you wrote on his cast," she said.

"I'll write whatever I want," I said, kicking my locker shut.

"When *I* signed his cast, our hands touched. Jared said, 'Does this mean we're going together?'" Her eyes glazed over. "Isn't that romantic?"

"This is too much," I whispered to myself. I could've told her those were his exact words to *me*.

Of course, she wouldn't believe me for a single second.

What a waste of time—sneaking out of the house, lying to Mom . . . getting grounded. Just to spend an afternoon with a complete jerk. I hurried down the hall, away from her.

"Holly, you owe me money for Bearie-O," Andie shouted after me. "The fur's worn off his head. I'll overlook it for a couple of tens."

I quickened my pace, ignoring her. I wasn't sure who I hated most—her or Jared.

♥   ♥   ♥

Tuesday night, Mom drove me to my first youth meeting. It was like my debut or something. Pastor Rob introduced me to all the kids. Everyone clapped. Danny and Alissa sat together, holding hands. Andie arrived late, and squeezed in beside Jared. I sat with some new kids.

After the meeting, I was heading down the hallway when Mr. Keller, the choir director, came out of his office.

"Holly!" he said. "You're just the person I was looking for."

He ushered me into his office and I sat down. He perched on the edge of his desk and explained that he needed an alternate singer for the tour to take the place of Alissa Morgan, who was moving.

"You have a fine voice, Holly, but I didn't choose you earlier because you were a bit younger and I thought I should give the older kids a chance first. However, now that Alissa is leaving, we need you. Can you attend all the rehearsals and catch up a little at home, as well?"

To sing in this choir I'd do anything! But then I remembered Daddy and his airplane tickets. I hesitated.

"Is there a problem?" he asked.

"Might be," I said, still surprised at this fabulous turn of events. "How soon do you have to know?"

"Two days. There are kids who would trade places with you in a flash."

Climbing into the car, after the meeting, I told Mom the fantastic news. "What'll I do?" I moaned. "Will Daddy understand if I don't go to see him?"

"You'll have to decide for yourself," she said.

Carrie piped up. "You don't *really* know him anyway."

"Speak for yourself," I shot back.

"Please, girls," Mom scolded. Then she said, "Holly-Heart, what about talking to the Lord about it?"

Praying. Hmm. Something I should've thought of.

At home, I went to my room and knelt at my window seat. It felt good talking to God about everything. Again.

Then I thought about Daddy. I needed to tell *him* about the choir tour as well. Mom was tucking Carrie into bed, so I went into her room to use the phone.

It rang four times. When I heard his voice, I said, "Daddy, it's Holly. Something's come up." I told him about the choir tour opening.

"That's wonderful news." He sounded excited.

"There's only one problem," I said.

"What's that?"

"The tour is during spring break."

There was a short pause. "I guess we could plan your visit for another time." Disappointment had leaped into his voice.

"What about this summer?" I suggested.

"That's a possibility." His voice revved up a bit.

"The choir's coming to California. Maybe you could come to hear us sing."

"You can count on it. We'll be there."

We'll. That meant I'd have to share him with Saundra. Even the way he pronounced her name gave me the creeps. Could prayer change my attitude towards her?

I wandered downstairs, looking for Mom. She was in the family room, curled up reading a book. "Where's Carrie's last report card?" I asked.

"In the desk in my room." She looked puzzled. "Why do you want it?"

I sat down beside her on the couch. "I thought Carrie could send it to Daddy. I feel funny about Carrie being left out of things with him. She's his daughter, too."

"How does *she* feel about it?" Mom asked, reaching over to loosen the pink barrettes in my hair.

"I'm not sure. I hope she doesn't feel jealous. Jealousy is a miserable thing."

"Well, now that he's shown an interest again,

maybe she'll get used to the idea of reaching out to him, too."

She brushed one side of my hair, while I did the other.

"Why didn't he keep in touch with us more than just a note on a birthday card or tons of presents at Christmas?" This question burned inside me.

"Honey, I don't understand that either. But I *do* know he has paid his support money to the court registry faithfully every month all these years."

She braided my hair in one thick braid.

"It's still hard," I said, deep in thought, "but I'm more concerned with his salvation now." It was true. Very few nights had passed recently that I didn't say his name in my prayers.

"I feel very close to you tonight," Mom said, giving me a hug.

"I feel it too." I felt sorry for Stan, Phil, Mark, and little Stephie. "Mom?" I said, thinking of their loss.

"Yes, honey?"

"I really do love you. Always remember?"

"I'll remember." She hugged and kissed me, and I headed for bed.

♥　　♥　　♥

At Wednesday night choir rehearsal, I was assigned a spot on the risers . . . beside Jared! I felt like smashing his sweet face in, but I kept my hands firmly gripped on the music folder.

"What a relief," Jared said between the first and second songs. "You're here. It's like a miracle."

"The only miracle I know is you haven't been found out before now," I blurted out.

"What do you mean, Holly-Heart?" He sounded so innocent.

"Don't call me that." I felt sick inside. Crushed. And fooled—into thinking he was too good to be true.

We practiced five more songs for our tour repertoire before Mr. Keller dismissed us. Andie came right over to Jared, ignoring me. She acted like a mother hen, holding his crutches, helping him with his coat.

I couldn't watch this. In the strongest voice I could muster I said, "Jared, you're not welcome at my birthday party. I've thought about this a lot, and I'm sorry." Heading for the church foyer, I waited for Mom, holding my breath, and willing the tears away.

Thursday morning I got up early. Quietly, I pulled a purple folder out from between the box springs and mattress of my canopy bed. I had told Andie about destroying our original Loyalty Papers, but she didn't know there was another copy.

It was time to confront Andie with the truth about Jared. I cut out the paragraph referring to one of us backing away from a guy to save our friendship. In a bright pink marker, I circled it and wrote, "I'm willing. Jared's not worth the destruction of us!"

There, that should speak loud and clear. I folded it neatly and slipped it into a business-sized envelope. Licking it shut, I labeled the envelope,

IMPORTANT! PRIVATE! I would lay it in her gym locker during warm-ups.

With my birthday party only three days away, things had to work out between Andie and me. And soon.

FIFTEEN

On the snowy walk to school, I kept thinking about Andie. Would she accept my note? What could I do to make her see what a two-timer Jared was?

I was heading up the sidewalk to school when I heard someone call my name. I turned.

It was Jared. He sat on the brick wall surrounding the courtyard leading to the main entrance of Dressel Hills Junior High. He had his bum leg sticking out, supported by one crutch. In his hand lay a single, long-stemmed rose.

"Holly," he called again. "This is for you." He held it out.

"Give it to Andie," I said.

He ignored that. "I know it's late, Holly, but happy birthday. And . . . I'm sorry about your aunt."

"Not sorry enough." I folded my arms.

"I know what you're thinking," he said. "But things aren't the way they seem." He shifted his bad leg off the crutch.

"You must think I'm real dense, Jared. I really don't want any of your explanations. What you did was heartless. I thought you were better than that." I turned to go.

"Honestly, Holly, Andie and I are *just friends*," he insisted, holding the rose out further.

"Is that what you told her about me? Where is she anyway?"

Jared frowned. "What's the matter, Holly?"

"Nothing's wrong with me. You're the one with a problem." I remembered, with a twinge of pain, how perfect things were . . . just a week ago, *before* I'd left for Aunt Marla's funeral. The outside temperature added to the cold, painful reality of seeing Jared for who he really was. I shivered, pulling the collar of my coat against my neck.

"C'mon, Holly." He held the sweet-smelling rose out to me again. "I want you to have this." It was hard to resist.

"Don't do this," I pleaded. I left him sitting alone. As I went throught the front doors of the school, I didn't look back.

During P.E., I slipped back into the girls' locker room. Quickly, I opened my locker and found the long envelope with the copy of the clipping from the Loyalty Papers. I hurried to Andie's locker and slid the envelope through the slits in the door. *Now* she'd have something to think about. Maybe

131

she'd even call me and request a face-to-face meeting. I was desperate to get my best friend back!

After school, I noticed Jared in the stairwell. He'd cornered some girl; I couldn't see who. But it wasn't Andie. Whoever it was, I could tell they were involved in animated conversation.

Way to go, Jared. Try and fool someone new. Peering around the corner at them made me hurt all over again.

Billy Hill zipped past, nearly knocking me over. "Excu-use me," he said. Together we walked towards the front entrance. "You look depressed."

"It's Jared. Mr. Flirt himself is trying his charm on yet another girl," I said, referring to the stairwell scene. "Why did *I* fall for it?"

"Don't go getting down on yourself," Billy said, "He can't be thinking straight."

"Now he's two-timing Andie. If she only knew!"

"If I were Jared, I'd stick with Andie," he said, and then, realizing he'd let something personal slip, he blushed.

He likes Andie! I thought. Perfect. I shifted my books from one arm to the other.

"The way Jared was talking in class, you'd think he was stringing you along, too." Billy was covering his tracks.

I scuffed my shoe as hard as I could. "His brain's definitely warped."

Just then a fabulous idea struck. "Wouldn't it be

fun to catch Jared at his own game? You know, teach him a lesson?"

"Yeah," Billy laughed. "Sure would!"

We pushed the front doors open. The smell of woodsmoke filled the air.

"Let's talk later," I said. We headed home in opposite directions.

Cutting through the school yard, I noticed Marcia Greene making fresh footprints in the snow. She wore a heavy tan parka. The hood was tied tightly, framing her face, and in her mittened hand she had a single long-stemmed red rose.

So *that's* who he'd cornered back there! Marcia Greene and I were destined for a heart-to-heart talk. Andie, too. Wait'll *she* heard about this . . . precisely what I needed to convince her of the truth. I decided to wait until after supper to call— it would give her a chance to get finished with homework before I dumped this on her.

When I got home, Carrie had stacks of art work and old report cards piled on the table. She must've heard about my chat with Mom last night.

"Carrie," I called, opening the fridge.

She bounded up the stairs and into the kitchen. "You're home!"

"How would you like to make a little package to send to Daddy?"

She showed off two pages of art work. "These are my favorites. Think he'll like them?"

I nodded. "If you want to keep these, we'll ask Mom to make copies at work."

Carrie liked that idea. I spent the rest of the afternoon helping her compose a letter to Daddy.

After a supper of chicken chow mein, I settled down at the dining room table to do some homework. I had just finished my algebra assignment when the phone rang. I flew across the kitchen to get it.

"Hi, Holly." It was Billy.

"What's up?"

"I was thinking about what you said today. I saw this show on TV about a guy who wasn't happy unless he was dating at least two girls at once."

"And?"

"He not only two-timed every girl he went with, but he got messed up trying to keep things straight with the girls he had lined dates up with."

"That won't happen to Jared," I said, "not when the word about him gets out to every girl in Dressel Hills. Beginning with Andie." I took a deep breath. "I have a fabulous scheme. Wanna help me pull it off?"

"No prob," Billy said.

"Here it is." I told him what I'd dreamed up on my way home from school.

Billy laughed when he heard my plan. "You're right!" he said. "Your birthday party will be the perfect place to set Jared up."

"Good. Talk to you later," I said, excitement jitters building inside.

After I hung up, I grabbed my notebook of

secret lists. There were important details to plan, involving Andie, Marcia Greene, and Jared.

First, I called Marcia Greene. She was hesitant, maybe a teeny bit taken in by Jared's attention, but willing to go along with the plan . . . for a price. I had to let her wear my purple and pink jacket to some ski party next week.

I agreed.

Next, I called Jared. He seemed surprised but thrilled that I'd changed my mind about including him at the party. I didn't tell him *who* was coming, of course.

Getting Andie to come to my party would be more difficult. I called her last.

"Hi, Andie. It's Holly. Please don't hang up," I said.

"What can *you* possibly say worth listening to?" she said sarcastically.

Praying for courage, I said, "Andie, I really want you to come to my party Saturday night."

She hesitated. "Uh, I don't know."

"Did you find the note I stuck in your locker with the clipping from the Loyalty Papers?" I persisted. "Did you read it?"

"Sort of, but I'm not—"

"*Jared's* coming to the party. I thought you'd want to come with him." It was my last ploy.

"Sure, I'll be there. But don't expect me to share him."

I stifled the urge to do backflips. "Perfect," I said, "I'll see you Saturday night."

We said good-bye. Then I clenched my fists and

jumped up and down. Mom looked at me funny when she came through the room hauling the vacuum cleaner and its attachments.

"A major accomplishment," I said, picking up the long vacuum hose. "Here, let me help."

"Looks like we have spiders again," Mom said, waving her feather duster in the corner of the ceiling and whisking away a few cobwebs.

I shivered at the thought of the creepy things. "I don't see any spiders now," I said, fluffing up the sofa pillows.

"Not now maybe, but the proof's in the webs they spin."

It sounded like a bit of poetry and reminded me of the mini-web of lies I hoped to spin for Andie this Saturday night—lies that would help her to see the truth.

Friday after school Billy and I walked to my house.

"Your plan to expose Jared is so cool," he said, stomping the snow off his boots.

"If each of us does his part, it should come off like vanilla pudding." Then I set things straight with Billy. "This whole thing is *not* about revenge, you know. It's about getting my best friend back."

"There's no way it won't work. You'll have Andie back tomorrow night, you'll see." His smile was so big I was curious about *his* motive.

At choir rehearsal Saturday morning I went out of my way to be nice to Jared. It wasn't easy. After all, I had been madly in love with him last week. The wound was still fresh.

"Thanks for inviting me to your party, Holly," he said, sliding over on the riser to make room for me. "I thought you didn't want me to come."

"I changed my mind." I didn't say I'd had a change of heart—that would have been lying.

Mr. Keller chose several kids to sing in an a cappella group. Danny Myers was one of the tenors. I listened as they sang, admiring Danny's performance.

After choir, Mr. Keller congratulated us on our good blend. "When we achieve unity with our voices, our music is that much stronger—more powerful. The same is true in our Christian life: when as brothers and sisters in Christ, we have unity of mind and heart, we can accomplish more for his kingdom."

I thought about his words. Even though we were both Christians, there hadn't been much unity between Andie and me lately. I hoped my plan would help restore some of that unity—and give me back my best friend.

SIXTEEN

Pastel streamers and paper cut-outs dangled from the ceiling of the dining room, creating a festive atmosphere. The table was covered with Mom's special lace tablecloth. Pink napkins were lined up beside pink plastic bowls. The middle of the table was covered with ten kinds of ice-cream toppings: strawberries, caramel, butterscotch, hot fudge, chocolate sprinkles, nuts, gummy bears, sliced bananas, maraschino cherries, and—best of all—whipped cream.

Mom rearranged the silverware. "We're all set, Holly-Heart," she said. "Why don't you go get yourself ready?"

I stood back and surveyed the table. "It's beautiful, absolutely beautiful." Impulsively, I hugged Mom. "Thanks."

138

"Hurry along, now," she said, chuckling like it was *her* party!

I charged upstairs and slipped into my new designer jeans and a hot-pink turtleneck with tiny white hearts on the neck and cuffs. Then I went into the bathroom to fix my hair. I brushed it vigorously, then curled and sprayed my bangs.

At 7:00 sharp, the doorbell rang. I ran downstairs and greeted my first guests, Joy and Shauna, two girls from my home ec class. Two boys from the basketball team showed up next. Later, Jared and Andie arrived. I smiled and welcomed them, but they couldn't look me in the eye. I offered them seats in the living room, where the other kids waited for the ice cream bonanza.

The doorbell rang again. I hurried to get it.

"Billy!" I gasped. "What happened to you?"

Billy, his right leg in a cast and crutches under his arms, wobbled into the living room. Marcia Greene followed, watching him and holding his arm so he wouldn't slip.

Everyone circled Billy, firing questions at him. "Clear the way," I said. "Let him sit down." I led Billy to a chair and propped his leg on a footstool.

"How does that feel?" I asked, sneaking a look at Jared. He was sitting next to Andie on the couch, a puzzled look on his face.

"It was a skiing accident," Billy told us. "Yesterday morning. I was skiing fast down a black slope when I hit this mogul and boom—I was gone." He described with delight how his sister had screamed and how the ski patrol had taken him

139

down on the snowmobile. "Lucky my mom's a doctor. She made sure I didn't go into shock and freeze to death," he said.

I stole another look at Jared. He was listening to Billy with interest. *Good,* I thought. *So far, so good.*

"Ice cream's ready," Mom called. We all trooped into the kitchen, where Mom told us what flavors were available. We lined up at the kitchen bar, and Mom dished out the ice cream. Then we circled the dining room table and picked out our favorite toppings.

Andie hovered near Jared. "What ice cream would you like?" she asked. "I can get it for you."

Marcia did the same. "Oh, Billy," she said. "Just tell me what you'd like on your sundae, and I'll take care of it."

A few minutes later Andie picked up the can of whipped cream. "Would you like some?" she asked Jared.

When she finished with the can, Marcia reached for it. "Billy," she said, her voice a tad sweeter than Andie's, "would you like some of this?"

"Please," he said, hamming it up.

Andie turned pink. Jared frowned.

We stood around the dining room, laughing and talking as we ate our huge sundaes. After we finished, Billy motioned for me.

Balancing on his crutches, he held his pink punch cup high. "Here's to the birthday girl," he said. Then he leaned over and brushed a kiss against my cheek. I giggled and pretended to enjoy it. All part of the act. Jared's eyes nearly popped out.

After seconds of ice cream, we went downstairs to the family room while Mom and Carrie cleared away the dishes. Tossing our shoes off, we curled up on the sectional facing the entertainment center and started a video. On the coffee table stood a tall white vase displaying a single, long-stemmed rose—which I had bought myself that afternoon.

The movie was one of my favorites—*Man from Snowy River*. So romantic. But I hardly paid attention. I kept watching Andie and Jared. The room was dark, but I thought I saw them holding hands. I bit the ends of my hair, nervous about what Billy and I had schemed to do.

The end of the video was Billy's cue. As soon as I rewound the movie and turned on the lights, he whipped out a blue marker and asked everyone to sign his cast. When Marcia signed it, LOVE, MARCIA G., he grabbed her hand and said, "Does this mean we're going out?"

She stuttered, acting the part flawlessly. "I–I'll have to ask Jared," she said, facing the former love of my life.

There was a long, awkward silence.

Then Andie leaped up. "What's going on?" she shouted, frowning at me, then glaring at Marcia. "Jared and *I* are together. What's this about?"

By now, Jared looked like a trapped rat. An almost speechless one. He mumbled, "I–uh–I don't . . ."

Marcia stared at Jared and poured it on. "I

thought we were going out. Isn't that what the rose was for?"

Andie let out a tiny gasp. She swung around to face Jared, cheeks pink with anger. I'd never known Andie to be tongue-tied, but at this minute, she was absolutely silent.

Now, it was *my* turn. I picked up the dainty rosebud vase. Holding it high, I said, "Roses are usually given to show love. This rose is like the one Jared wanted to give me. But I refused it." I looked at Andie, hoping she could see my demonstration of loyalty.

"He gave one to *me*, too," Marcia declared, "after school."

"This is nuts!" Andie looked from Marcia to me and back again. "I'm outta here." Her eyes shot fire. At me. "Holly, meet me upstairs," she said coldly. It sounded like an invitation to duel.

I followed her upstairs to the hall closet, where she dragged out her coat and put it on. Then she pulled me outside into the bitter night. Standing on the front porch, lit only by the dim glow of a distant streetlight, we faced each other.

"What are you trying to prove, Holly *Heartless*?" she asked, her arms folded.

"Only that I'm sick of Jared coming between us," I said. "I honestly thought this was the only way to show you what he was like. I doubt that Jared would tell you that he tried to give me a rose, then gave it to Marcia instead. He's a two-timer, Andie."

"I don't care!" she said.

"You're actually going to stick with Jared?"

She just glared at me.

"What about our friendship?" I asked, hoping. Hoping.

"It's over. You humiliated me, Holly." Her voice was shaking, and I thought I saw tears glistening in her eyes. "Our friendship's over. No more Loyalty Papers, no more teddy bears, no more nothing. You can forget about me, Holly Heartless, because this is the last time I'll ever set foot in your house."

Before I could say anything she had darted off, running full speed down our driveway and into the street.

"Andie!" I called. It was a long, cold three blocks to her house, but she didn't turn. Her figure rounded the corner and disappeared at the end of Downhill Court.

I shivered uncontrollably. My fabulous plan had backfired. I had just lost my best friend.

SEVENTEEN

Downstairs in the family room, I found the boys cutting through Billy's cast with a hacksaw I'd hidden behind the TV.

"Guess I won't need this now," Billy said, tossing the cast aside.

"Where'd you get it?" Joy asked.

"My mother's a doctor. She did a good job of making me look like a real crip."

Staring at the signatures on the discarded cast, I felt sick inside. The scheme had blown up in my face. And Andie and I were as far removed as the east is from the west.

Jared? He was missing.

"He's hiding in the bathroom," Billy said when I asked. "We sure did a number on him."

"It wasn't him we were after," I whispered,

wishing this night had never happened. It was obvious the party was over. I thanked Marcia Greene for her fabulous dramatic display as she left the house. Billy, too.

I vented my frustration by heading back to the family room and yanking down the streamers. At last, Jared came out of the bathroom, like a turtle emerging from its shell.

He picked up the vase with the rose and leaned his nose deep into the flower. "It's too bad, isn't it?" he said.

I tossed a crumpled wad of crepe paper to the floor. "You're not kidding."

Jared continued. "A rose is a symbol of love. The Bible says we should love everyone. Right? I'm doing the best I can to be a loving Christian."

I wanted to choke. Was this guy for real?

"Jared Wilkins, go home. You're leading girls on and that has nothing to do with God's love." I threw his coat at him and pointed to the stairs.

He flashed me a wink and a grin. "See you, Holly-Heart."

He never gives up, I thought as I hurried to find Mom. She was in bed, propped up in pillows and reading a magazine. When she saw me, she patted the bed beside her. I snuggled beside her on the pillows and unloaded the entire dreadful evening on her.

"You humiliated Andie in front of her classmates," Mom chided. "How else would you expect her to react?"

I nodded. "It was a lousy mistake. I didn't think

about how *she'd* feel, only how I was feeling about losing her friendship." I pulled my socks off and threw them one at a time across the room. "What should I do now?"

Mom slipped her arm around me. "Only one thing, Holly-Heart. Apologize."

She was right. "It won't be easy," I said. "And Andie might not forgive me."

Mom squeezed my hand. "You might be surprised."

I returned to my own bedroom, where I dressed in my nightshirt and read my devotional. Lying in the darkness, I replayed the events of the party in my mind. Over and over, I recalled Andie's reaction. How could she ever forgive me?

♥   ♥   ♥

During church the next day my conscience haunted me. How could I have done such a terrible thing to my best friend? I listened carefully when our pastor talked about forgiveness of sins, and said a silent prayer of thanks to God that he had already forgiven me. Now if I could only get Andie to do the same.

I searched for Andie after the service. Finally I found her alone in the choir practice room. She sat at the piano, numbering measures in her music.

I stood behind the piano, silent for a moment. Then I said, "I'm sorry about last night, Andie. Will you forgive me?"

She looked up, a hint of sadness in her eyes.

"Sure, Holly. I forgive you. But you should know that Jared and I are already back together."

I should've known. Jared's charm was hard to resist.

She went on. "He apologized to me, too. And to Marcia Greene. Jared's trying to be more up-front with me now. He just wants to be good friends with *all* the girls. Really."

Some joke. If only she knew Jared had flirted with *me* last night after everyone left. She'd never believe that!

I sighed. "That's good. I hope you guys get along okay." Then I turned and left the room. At least we were talking. But I knew we wouldn't be best friends again—not until Jared Wilkins was out of the picture.

February fizzled and March piled snow on us until I thought winter would never end. I spent most of my time with Marcia Greene. Even though Andie and I didn't talk much, at least we were civil to each other. She continued to help Jared with his crutches and his books, standing sentinel at his locker to assist him with his every whim.

The second week in March Jared had his cast removed. To celebrate, Andie decorated his locker door with balloons. I congratulated Jared, hoping now that he could walk without crutches, I'd get Andie back. But nothing changed. She stuck as close to Jared as before.

And worse—Jared kept flirting. At choir practices, in English class, at church. Even though I didn't respond, he kept it up.

At last it was Saturday, March 27—the final choir rehearsal before we left for our tour on Monday. After top-notch practices in February, the choir had gone into a slump, but Mr. Keller was going to present a unified choir or die trying.

We prayed at the beginning of the rehearsal, as usual. Then he said, "Let's chat." He motioned for us to sit on the risers. "Some of you are still thinking in terms of solo work. In a choir situation," and here he waved his arms to include all of us, "I must have togetherness. We're a group of singers, not thirty different people doing our own thing. So blend. Listen to each other. The theme of our tour is Hearts in One Accord. When we sing in each church, people must feel our inspiration, our love for the Lord, and for each other." A couple kids snickered. "You know what I mean," he said.

I glanced at Andie, at the piano. She was gazing at Jared, next to me. *She must think she's in love,* I thought sadly.

Mr. Keller wasn't finished. "Acts 2:46 says, 'Every day they continued to meet together in the temple courts. They broke bread in their homes and ate together with glad and sincere hearts, praising God and enjoying the favor of all the people.'" He asked for hands. "Let's have some input from you. What's this verse saying?"

Hands shot up.

"Yes, Danny?"

"The Christians were in agreement. They were united."

"Exactly," Mr. Keller said. "More ideas?" He pointed to Jared.

"They looked forward to pigging out together?" The kids laughed.

Mr. Keller nodded. "But wasn't it more *how* they did it?"

I raised my hand. "They were together in everything. Like best friends."

"Now we're getting somewhere," he said, rubbing his hands together. "Think about what Holly said as we rehearse the last stanza of page 44."

I thought about Andie sitting at the piano as we sang. More than anything I hoped this choir tour would restore us to true friendship.

EIGHTEEN

Dizzy with excitement, I stood at the back of the Los Angeles Chapel, peering through the glass that separated the foyer from the sanctuary. I saw scarcely a vacant seat, each one filled, right up to the altar. The crowd fidgeted. Young children peeked at parents' programs, teens whispered on the far left side, segregated from the rest. I looked over rows of heads and soon spied the red, swept-up hair of Saundra. Where was Daddy?

I became aware of the nervous rustlings behind me—the other girls, straightening their tea-length apricot-colored dresses.

"Ready for this?" Jared, my escort, whispered.

I caught a glimpse of Daddy at the drinking fountain. "Excuse me," I said, moving out of line and dashing to him.

"Holly," he said with awe in his voice. "Holly, you look simply stunning." He gave me a tight hug.

I heard the cue and reluctantly pulled away. "Wait for me after the concert." I scurried back to my appointed spot.

Jared's hand touched my back lightly as he guided me to my place beside him. I slipped my hand through his elbow and we were off. It felt weird walking down the aisle with Jared, like we were in a wedding, or worse, getting married to each other! Andie regarded us with a half-sarcastic, half-accusing look as we rounded the altar and up the steps.

On the platform, we located our place on the risers. I searched the audience. Daddy was leaning forward slightly. His warm smile beckoned to me like a beacon in the sea of faces.

Energetically, we sang our opening song, a lively chorus, "Everybody Sing Praises to the Lord." It was a great start by the sound of the applause. Somehow, I made it through the next few songs, even though Jared kept inching closer and closer. He and Andie had worked out some exclusive thing between them, and I refused to respond to his flirting.

At the intermission, during the offering, Jared strolled through the lobby to me. Handsomely outfitted in his black tux with ruffled apricot-colored shirt, he was any girl's dream.

"You're going to introduce me to your father, aren't you?" he asked, grinning flirtatiously.

I stepped back. "Why should I?"

"C'mon, Holly, you know Andie and I are just—"

"I've heard it before, Jared. Just friends, right?" I interrupted.

Andie materialized out of nowhere. "Flirting again, I see." She said it to *me*.

"Look at Jared when you say that. If you're too blind to see the truth, then you deserve him!" I hurried to the back of the foyer area. Refusing to cry, I flipped through the church's brochure, pretending to read the now blurry statement of faith.

"Holly?"

Whirling around, I found the grey-green eyes of Danny Myers looking at me.

"Problems with Andie?" His voice had a calming effect on me. I didn't have to tell him what was wrong. The whole choir knew by now.

My voice grew soft, "It's not her fault. She's just . . ."

"Just what?" He seemed interested. His eyes were kind—so was his face. He was older than me and more spiritual—I remembered that from the way he'd prayed even at school during lunch.

"She's been fooled," I finally said. "It makes me angry."

"Why does that bother you so much?"

I told him how close Andie and I had always been—until now. How I preferred *one* best friend and Andie had changed all that, because of Jared.

Danny nodded and smiled like he understood.

"Sit here, Holly." He patted a chair near the deacon's room. "You can't sing with these feelings. You're here to minister through music. There could be people needing to hear about Jesus."

"Yes, I know," I said, tears refusing to dry up. I was thinking of one of those people. Daddy. This gospel message we sang was for him. "I can't go back in there at all," I mumbled through my tissue. "Not looking this way."

"Let me pray for you, Holly."

I blinked the stubborn tears away.

"Let's pray for Andie, too," he said. "She *needs* your friendship again. Can you forgive her?"

"In my heart, I can. Outside, it's not so easy."

Danny prayed a quiet prayer, full of total assurance. It touched my heart. As we lined up for the second half, I felt confident again.

I thrilled to the melodies we sang—slow hymns and fast gospel songs. Lost in the music, I watched Mr. Keller's every move. During the last song, I saw Daddy reach for his handkerchief. He wiped his eyes. It was the first time I'd seen him cry. A lump came in my throat. Could this concert be a new beginning for him? The answer to my prayers?

The church was nearly empty by the time the equipment was carried out to the bus. Daddy and I were still talking in the second row. Saundra had politely disappeared a half hour before.

Daddy held my hand as he spoke. "So much about me has changed since your Aunt Marla died. Losing her has been a great shock. And losing four years of your life . . . and Carrie's, well, I just want to catch up somehow."

I hugged him, the tears dripping onto his suit coat. He gave me his handkerchief.

"I've been praying for you all this time," I said.

"And I love you for it," he said, holding both my hands in his. "We'll have lots more to discuss when you visit this summer." Another quick hug. "Holly? Please tell Carrie I love her, too."

"Those words should come from you," I said.

"The right time will come." He dug into his pocket and pulled two twenty-dollar bills from his clip. "Here, spend this at Disneyland tomorrow."

Something stirred in me. It was the question I had never asked him: Why had he abandoned us? My lips formed the words, but my heart squelched them. I mustn't spoil this moment.

"Thanks, Daddy," I said, staring at the money. I loved *him*, not what he could give me.

"I'll call you when you get back from tour," he said.

"Okay," I answered. One last quick hug, and he was gone.

Staring at the empty pew beside me, I wondered why things had to be this way. If only Daddy hadn't remarried. I crossed my arms and bent over, hugging myself. The old, familiar ache of his absence had returned.

NINETEEN

The towering pinnacles of Sleeping Beauty's Castle loomed into view as our bus rumbled to a stop near the entrance to the Magic Kingdom. Mr. Keller gave some last minute instructions. "Above all," he warned, "remain in twos. Girls with girls, and boys with boys. Go with your partner everywhere."

Danny flashed a grin at me. I knew he was saying, *Go for it, Holly. Forgive your friend.* Most girls would have loved to have an attractive older brother-type treating them the way Danny treated me. He was perfect.

I leaned over the seat behind Andie. "Wanna be my partner?

"Why not," she grumbled. "Everyone else has one."

Inside, we raced to Splash Mountain first. The line was long. Just hearing the screams of delight (or was it terror?) as the kids came hurtling down the fifty-foot drop-off, doing forty miles an hour in those little log boats, told us it would be worth the wait in the hot sun.

Here I was waiting in line to go on a fabulous ride at Disneyland with my former best friend, and we weren't talking. She was being a real pain about it, too, keeping her face turned away from me.

I opened my backpack filled with pop, munchies and a jacket in case of rain. "Want a soda?" I asked.

"Is it warm?" she asked.

"Not yet. Here, feel." I held it out.

"That's okay," she said. "Save my place, I'll get my own."

My heart sank. What more could I do? Was I trying too hard?

My journal was tucked away in one corner of my backpack. While Andie ran off to get a cold pop, I wrote Proverbs 17:17 in my secret notebook. "A friend loves at all times." *Hmm,* I thought, *that means I should keep showing Andie I care about her, even though she's being so snooty.*

Shortly, Andie was back. With a hot dog, chips, and pop. She ignored me worse than ever, talking to the girl *behind* us, instead of me.

Forty-five minutes later, we staggered out of the log boat, having just flown down Chickapin Hill and survived.

"Wanna go again?" I asked, hoping for a response.

"Maybe later," was all she said.

Undaunted, I headed for the Matterhorn bobsleds. After a thrilling ride through the black depths of the mountain, and an unexpected encounter with the Abominable Snowman, Andie and I lined up for some spooky fun at the Haunted Mansion.

Then I spotted Jared. He was across from us, on the docks of the river rafts, sitting with his partner and sharing sodas with two sopranos. I watched as he worked his magic.

"Look over there," I said pointing at Andie's two-timing friend.

"What?" Andie turned. She spotted Jared with the girls, and her face fell.

In silence we watched as he teased one of the girls, a soprano named Amy-Liz. She was one of the cutest girls in seventh grade, with curly blonde hair and sparkling blue eyes. Jared's foot, newly released from its cast, reached out under the table and touched hers. She giggled and pulled back a little—but not too much. Then his foot found hers again.

"They're playing footsie!" Andie screeched. "I don't believe it!"

She ducked under the ropes holding us in line and marched over to Jared. Dying to hear what she would say, I followed.

"Yo, Jared!" she called.

He spun around, a guilty look on his face. But as

soon as he saw Andie he grinned, bowing low. "Andie, my lady."

"Cut the comedy act," she said. "What do you think you're doing?" She glared at Amy-Liz.

"Spreading Christian love," he said, the girls giggling behind him.

"Wrong answer. Try this: you're two-timing every girl, everywhere, all the time!"

"I kept telling you, Andie, we're just friends, right?" He turned to Amy-Liz. "Just like Amy-Liz and me." Laughing, he took her hand and they left the table.

"You just wait," Andie hollered back. "Every girl in Dressel Hills will hear about you. I promise!"

He waved without turning around.

"He should apply for the Disneyland court jester, don't you think?" I said.

There was disgust written all over her face. No tears, no jealousy, just plain old disgust. The light had dawned!

"Jared's out. He and I are through," she announced, studying me momentarily. "Holly, can you forgive me for everything? I mean, everything?"

I had been hoping, holding my proverbial breath for this moment. "Hallelujah! The loathsome nightmare is past and I've regained my long-lost best friend."

"Talk in English, would you?" she said, giggling. This was it. The old Andie was back.

"Look up there," I said pointing. "Let's celebrate at the Hungry Bear Restaurant." At once we raced up the wooden walkway. Waiting in line to order hamburgers, Andie turned me around and braided my hair.

When we finally sat down at a table on the banks of the Rivers of America, I noticed a lumpy bump in my backpack.

"What's this?" I investigated inside. Andie opened her bag of chips, ignoring me.

There, under my jacket, and all smashed up, was Andie's droopy-eyed teddy bear.

"Pals forever?" she said, wearing a sheepish grin.

"—until the very end of us," I quoted from our now defunct Loyalty Papers, hugging Bearie-O.

"He's missed you, you know," she said softly. "And so have I."

My emotions soared. "I missed you too," I said.

She took a bite of hamburger, her eyes shining. "You're really all heart, Holly. Honest. No one else would've stuck with me this long." She sprinkled salt on my fries.

"Believe me, I had major help," I said, glancing heavenward.

♥　　**About the Author**　　♥

Beverly Lewis remembers her "first love." He had light wavy hair and a heart-melting smile. And he attended the church her father pastored while she was growing up in Lancaster County, Pennsylvania.

Beverly's junior high P.E. teacher called her a nickname just as embarrassing as "Holly Bones." And best friends? She knows all about true-blue, *best*, best friends. Hers was Sandi Kline, and although they didn't have Loyalty Papers, they *did* write secret codes. Once they even hid some under the carpet of the seventh step leading to the sanctuary of her dad's church.

A former schoolteacher, Beverly has published over forty short stories and articles in magazines such as *Highlights for Children, Brio, Faith 'n Stuff, Dolphin Log*, and *Guide*. Her hilarious chapter books are titled *Mountain Bikes and Garbanzo Beans* and *The Six-Hour Mystery*.